HUNTED ON HALLOWEEN

A STANDALONE HOLIDAY PARANORMAL ROMANCE

MONSTERS OF THE DIVIDE
BOOK 4

T. B. WIESE

BOOKS IN THIS WORLD

- Paine for the Holidays
- A Vexing Valentines
- A Malicious Summer Vacation
- Hunted on Halloween

For everyone who fantasizes about being chased through the woods ...
It's time to sink your teeth into spooky season.

AUTHOR'S NOTE

**Please take care of yourself and your mental health

Hunted on Halloween is an ADULT paranormal romance that contains elements such as: monsters, violence, swearing, borderline non-con, blood, fire, being burned, biting, claiming, chasing, and sexually explicit scenes ... with monsters.

HAUNTING HALLOWEEN COCKTAIL

(https://www.bbcgoodfood.com/recipes/halloween-cocktail)

Ingredients

- ice cubes
- 125ml black vodka, or use Crème de cassis and a touch of black food colouring, but it will be much sweeter
- 100ml vodka
- 250ml pomegranate juice (we used Pom)
- 4 dashes orange bitters
- 8 blackberries
- pomegranates, to serve (optional)

To garnish the glasses

- 1 tbsp honey or golden syrup
- black sanding sugar, or black cake decorating sprinkles

Directions

Rim of four martini glasses with honey and black sugar or sprinkles.

Fill a large cocktail shaker with a big handful of ice cubes and pour in the black vodka, vodka, pomegranate juice, and bitters. Shake and divide among the glasses. Thread the berries on cocktail skewers and place one in each cocktail. To make it even more haunting, drop some pomegranate seeds in the drink

MONSTERS OF THE DIVIDE

*Most of these are only briefly mentioned in passing, so don't feel too overwhelmed.

Ancients - Oldest of the monsters. No one knows where they came from or what their original form looks like. They shapeshift into any form. Extremely powerful. Respected and feared by all. Very reclusive.

Nepha - Humanoid with metallic feathered wings. These are the creatures Angles were modeled from. They are exceptional hunters - even our MMC is wary of them. They are beautiful but cruel. Most believe that if they have hearts, they are made of stone.

Dremar - Think vampire and gargoyle. This species has different colored skin. Our MMC has blue-grey skin that is smooth and hairless, but others have shades of red or green or black ... Eyes to match their skin color. Males and females have curly horns like an antelope. They are very fast on foot, even faster when flying. They have bat-like wings, a snake-like tail, fangs, and claws. They drink blood, not to survive, but to obtain power. They heal very quickly. Any being that they've tasted the blood of, they can incinerate with a thought. The dremar, but especially our MMC, are feared by other monsters.

Anza - Smaller comparatively in the monster realm - about the size of the average human female. They have shimmery skin like starlight. They are pretty and disarming. They are one of the fastest monsters, able to move so quickly they are a blur. They have sharp teeth, a hypnotizing gaze, and can secrete hallucinogens from their skin to incapacitate their prey, which they like to peel and eat. Death by anza is very slow and painful. Not only can they heal themselves, but they can heal others - if you can convince them to.

Xani - Scaled skin that is very tough. Hairless. Usually green but can be other colors. They have reflective, reptile-like eyes. Sharp teeth. Extremely fast. Can walk upright or on all fours. They have snake-like tails, and hate the light, always sticking to shadows unless the hunt of a prey brings them out.

Joteunn - Fur-covered like a werewolf, only they don't shift. They have wolf-like ears and a snout with sharp teeth and fangs. They are pretty large comparatively in the monster world and are extremely strong. They heal very quickly as long as they have the magic to do so. They occasionally run in packs but prefer to hunt solo (as most monsters do). They do howl and bark to communicate, though they also speak.

Grateslung - Snake-like creature with the bottom half of a snake, the top half looks like a gargoyle without wings.

Stone-like skin on the body, scaled skin on the lower half. Usually shades of grey or black but can be different colors. Their saliva is venomous, and they are very strong and fast.

Quilen - Tall, humanoid monster that's thin but muscled. They have branch-like horns that look too heavy to hold up. They are dark skinned with black eyes, long spindly fingers with claws. They aren't the fastest of monsters, but they are strong and can slip between shadows.

Grae - Feathered all over. Humanoid body with a sharp beak, eagle talons for feet, and wings for arms. They are not the smartest monster - they are more animalistic.

Hellhounds - Large dog-like creatures the size of a pony. They do not speak. They hunt in packs, but once their prey is caught, it's every hellhound for themselves. They are a little further down on the food chain in the monster realm, which is why they tend to stay in groups.

Unicorns - They look just like our myths. Horse-like creatures with a single horn. But these unicorns are carnivorous with serrated teeth, razor sharp hooves, and are so strong, they can cave in a monster's chest with one kick. Their horns also emit a strong electric shock that can incapacitate or even kill.

Menace - spider like monsters with blades for legs. Hairy. Can't see well. Relies on sound waves and sense of smell. They lay eggs like spiders and shoot webs.

Oulurs - humans call them Oni. Demon-like. Red or black skin with horns and tusks and pointed tails. They will eat anything. Monster. Human. Animal. Plant. Garbage ...

We might meet more monsters in the upcoming books in this series, but these are all the ones in this story.

Enjoy.

CHAPTER 1

THE SIXTY SECONDS THAT CHANGED THE WORLD

Monsters are real.

Seventy-two years ago, they came.

Supposedly, at first, everyone thought it was a hoax. But it didn't take long for the world to realize that what was happening was indeed real. You can still find old clips of videos people took on their phones that night.

The monsters came through what we now call The Divide—the invisible barrier that separated our realm from theirs. Apparently, all throughout history, the occasional monster would get through—those folktales of werewolves, vampires, and fae started from somewhere. But that night, they all just ... appeared. So many humans lost their lives. The monsters took what they wanted ... blood, bones, fear, souls. Weapons didn't work on most of them ... with their tough skin, scales, super speed, wings, regenerative healing ... The humans were no match. It was a bloodbath. Then, six hours after they appeared, they all just vanished.

The entire planet was still reeling from the attack when it happened the next night, and the next. Always at the same time. Always for six hours. It wasn't until almost a week of the occurrences that someone discovered that the first night the monsters came through, all time stood still for one full minute. Clocks ceased ticking, tides froze, the world stopped turning. No one noticed, because well, monsters. And no one really knows how life on earth survived the literal freezing of time. Time hasn't stopped again since that first night, but the monsters still come.

Humanity's saving grace came with the discovery of magic symbols with the power to keep the monsters out. Who discovered it? That truth is buried under wild conjectures, outlandish legends, and fantastical myths. So, who knows?

And here we are. Life goes on. We go about the monster-free hours almost as normally as before, as if we're trying to ignore the nightmare we know is coming with the fall of The Divide every day. But we all know ...

The monsters *are* coming, and if you want to survive, there are only three rules:

Make sure the correct symbols are carved deep into your threshold and every windowsill.

Be sure you recharge the symbols with a few drops of your blood at least once a month to keep the monsters out.

And whatever you do, don't go outside after the final curfew siren.

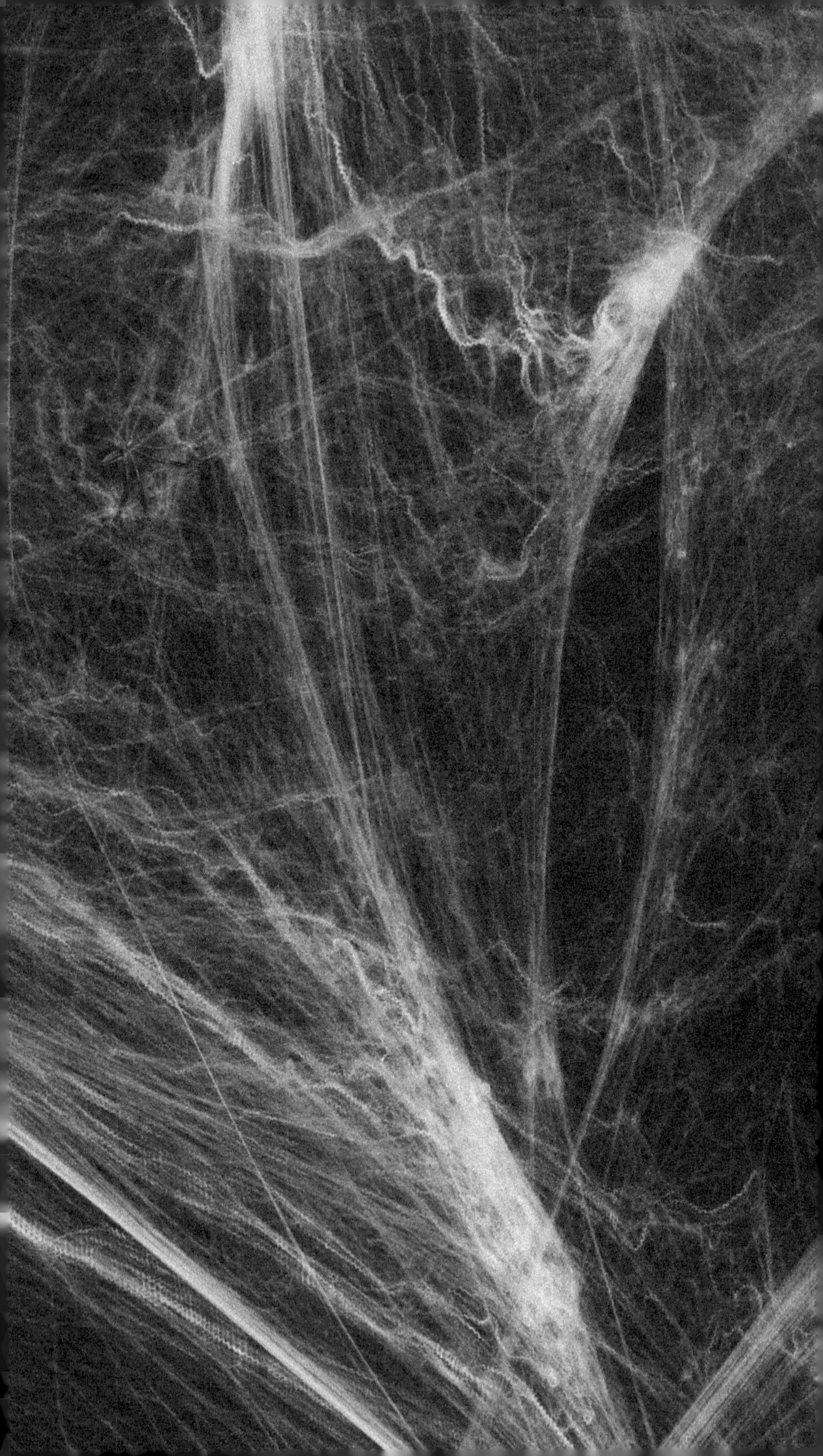

CHAPTER 2

THE ANCIENT

The dark jewel in my hand clinks against my claws, the resulting sound too pretty to come from such a soulless thing. The claws of my feet click against the stone floor as I cross the cavernous room containing my hoard. My foul mood lifts slightly as I glance at the glittering splendor all around me. Even after all these years, my shiny treasures bring me joy, each one attached to a memory—the gold church bell I took with me after I burned down that little human town, the pile of jewels I claimed after I defeated the fae prince in the realm of Stormfire, the gilded sword of one of the many vampire kings, a piece of the glowing star that sustained the magic of the people of the realm of ... I forget, but it was a glorious battle.

My tail trails behind me, swishing against the cold floor, and tendrils of comforting smoke swirl off me like a cloak. I shake off the stink of the human realm, cracking my neck. Even though it was late into the evening there, the summer heat still hung heavy in the air. It was sticky and unwelcome. I much prefer my realm, Ekenys. The monster realm is always cool since there's no sun to bake the earth, just blessed eternal night.

I avoid the human realm as much as possible. There are so many other delightful and interesting worlds to enjoy—not that I've left my mountain home to go anywhere in … decades. But tonight, I had no choice. Malicious, the winged nepha, just had to poke his nose where it didn't belong. That monster is like a cat … too curious for his own good.

A soft, *clink clink clink*, carries around the cave as I tap a claw to the black gem in my hand. Sure, the residual magic in this stone was drawing humans and their monster mates to its location—an ironic side effect that's not lost on me. But that didn't mean Malicious had to go and dig the jewel up, dredging these memories to the surface where I can't hide from them. I almost killed Malicious' human mate in my anger.

I'm still in my smaller form, not even twelve feet tall—including my many horns—which makes this cavern feel … empty. I'm used to my much larger form, what the humans would call a dragon. I use my physical presence to fill the spaces of my giant mountain home … trying to fill the void.

The jewel creaks and groans as I tighten my fist around it. With a growl, I squeeze tighter. "I can't believe you are still causing me trouble. I should crush you. I should grind you to powder and sprinkle you in my food, just so I can shit you out, then set you on fire." Relaxing my grip, I raise the gem to my face, whispering to its black facets. "I should have forgotten you by now."

The jewel fails to refract the light as I tilt it one way, then the other. Its dark depths pull a frown to my face.

"You should have slipped from my mind, from my memories. But I remember. I always have." Once again, my grip tightens. Just a bit more strength, and it will shatter.

I can't. I must wait. I will have my revenge.

With a growl, I toss the stone. It clatters with a musical sound as it lands on the giant slab table before me. I stare at it, waiting, straining to hear her voice, to see her golden eyes reflected from its black depths—for some sign that she has returned so I might destroy her all over again.

Nothing.

With a smirk, I bow low, sweeping my arms wide in a mocking gesture.

"Welcome to my home, you bitch. You're in Ekenys now. *My* realm. The realm of monsters where someone like you belongs. Make yourself comfortable, for this is where your black heart will reside for the rest of my immortal days."

Just be done with it. Get rid of it. Get rid of her. Crush it. Destroy it ... like she destroyed your heart.

My hand hovers over the gem, black curls of smoke coming off my skin, descending as if to caress its facets.

"DAMN IT!"

The walls shake with my bellow. A few pebbles tumble from the cave ceiling. Coins and treasures clink and clatter before the echo of my voice fades. The room settles, but that infuriating black jewel sits unbothered on the table, mocking me.

I spin, tempted to flick my tail to knock the stone to the floor in pettiness, but I leave it where it is ... in the dark, in the cold. Alone.

Like I have been since she betrayed me. Since the day I ripped her still beating heart from her chest, the day I watched the light leave her eyes and felt her heart turn to stone in my hand. Since the day she vowed with her dying breath to return.

Pausing, I look over my shoulder. My eyes easily find the black gem across the dark room. My whisper floats around the cavern, filling the space with my sorrow.

"I loved you."

Never again.

FOUR MONTHS LATER
ANA

The cafe lights strung back and forth across the street cast soft light on my dress, making the light green fabric sparkle. I do a little twirl, smiling with delight as my long, layered skirts swish around my legs. The lace bodice with delicate floral details hugs my waist and presses my small chest up into a hint of cleavage.

I look good.

I should with the amount of time I spent on this costume.

Someone bumps into me, and a few strands of my hair tug against my scalp as the flower crown on my head shifts to the left. I turn to face the bloody skeleton. He raises his hands with a wide smile. "Sorry. It's quite the turnout tonight, huh?"

I nod, looking around the packed street then back to the guy before me. His gaze traces from the intricate braids woven through my curly red hair to my slippered feet. He whistles, "Nice costume."

I don't miss the heat in his eyes, but I ignore it. I'm not here looking for anything ... certainly not a drunken Halloween hookup, no matter how long it's been. My vibrator does the job just fine, thank you very much.

Still, I am proud of my costume. With a smile, I flutter the skirts of my fairy dress, turning slightly to show off the iridescent wings strapped to my back. "Thanks."

He takes a step towards me, leaning in to be heard without yelling. "Is this innocent fairy here alone?"

The scents of beer and strong cologne assault me, and I fight to keep my nose from scrunching. Innocent? I may look so, but if he only knew the things I craved ... the things I read and secretly desire in my dark fantasy romances.

Luckily, I'm saved from this conversation when a shout pulls his attention from me.

"Hey! Brad! You made it. Awesome!"

A guy dressed in all leather, a bad fake wig, and shiny plastic fangs throws his arm around Brad the skeleton. The vampire hands Brad a red plastic cup, and a woman slides under Brad's arm on his other side. Her cat costume is tiiiight. *Is it painted on?* I'm tempted to glare at my small boobs as the cat woman presses her ample breasts against Brad. She trails her long black nails down his chest, not so subtly nudging him away from me.

Good. He's all yours, cat woman.

Skeleton Brad shoots me one more glance before his eyes lock on the cat woman's breasts, and he follows her into the press of bodies dancing in the street.

The music gets louder, the beat thumping through the air. The crowd yells, everyone throwing their hands up as they jump and dance to the music. Giant fake spider webs cover the bushes of the townhouses flanking either side of this street. Red lights shine from the porches, and candlelight flickers through a few windows.

I smile as I crouch, my skirts spreading around me. I read the inscription on one of the fake tombstones in the little yard of the blue townhouse.

Here lies Mary. She was always a bit scary. So leave her flowers so bright, to avoid a visit from her ghost in the night.

Chucking to myself, I read the next one.

Dear departed sister. Chased after the wrong mister. Caught by his wife. She met the end of her knife.

Yikes. Haha.

Scooting over slightly on my toes, I move to the next one.

Here lies Henry - a stalker and a creep. He did naughty things while women were asleep. so they removed his eyes and left him as a prize for the monsters who come at night ... much to their delight.

I chuckle. "Woah. Henry got what was coming to him."

I read the last one with a smirk on my face.

Dear sweet Lilly, beloved by all. Now in the ever after, probably having a ball.

I sigh. "Awe. Cute."

"What?"

The question draws my gaze up to the scarecrow man standing to my left. I wave a dismissive hand. "Nothing. Sorry."

He shrugs and moves deeper into the crowd. I smile as I turn back to the tombstones. I've always talked out loud to myself. I can't seem to keep my thoughts contained.

The music changes, and someone somewhere activates a smoke machine. I stand as the swirling mist swallows the concrete underfoot. My body vibrates with the beat, and I join the crowd, dancing with arms raised.

This Halloween block party is legendary in this town. Luckily, this time of year, it gets dark early enough to enjoy the spooky atmosphere before The Divide falls and we're all forced to hide away in our homes.

Hopping on the balls of my feet, I shake my hips as the weight of my wings pulls at my shoulders. I'm so grateful it's a mild night, though I would have braved the cold to keep from having to cover this beautiful fairy dress with a coat.

As I spin in place, I stop, my eyes bugging wide. A tall man dances a few feet away. He's painted from head to toe in dark blue paint. Giant horns curl from his head, and the leathery wings flaring from his back look so real, my fingers twitch with the urge to touch them. I can't even see the straps that hold those wings in place. Impressive. A beautiful woman dances in his arms, her head tilted back, her eyes on his face. The fuzzy white onesie she's wearing does nothing to hide her curvy figure, and the foam unicorn horn on her head bobs as she dances with the blue gargoyle man. Her silly costume paired with his realistic one is ... "cute."

Orange and purple strobe lights spear into the sky from the DJ booth as the song seamlessly changes. Once again, I get swept away by the atmosphere. The press of bodies and my exuberant dancing have me feeling flush.

I stumble slightly as a woman in tight scrubs bumps into me. She sways, the drink in her hand sloshing over the rim. With a drunk smile, she raises her cup in a salute as she shouts over the noise. "Sorry!"

I wave her off and keep dancing. She sweeps her free hand at me. "Great dress!"

"Thanks!"

She rocks back dangerously far but manages to right herself. I look around. *Is she alone?*

I'm not drinking because none of my friends could come tonight. And you don't go out drinking any time close to the fall of The Divide without a battle buddy—someone who will make sure you get to safety before the monsters come.

Though some people are just careless.

A few years ago, at this very block party, a man passed out in the bushes, and no one noticed. He didn't survive the night.

Just as I lean in to ask the sexy nurse if she is here with anyone, another woman leaps on her back, wrapping her arms around her neck. She plants a kiss on her cheek, then snatches the nurse's drink, swallowing the rest of the contents in one go. The two get swallowed by the crowd as they search for fresh drinks.

A man with impressive bronze angel wings spins a woman wearing a white dress and halo. She giggles, and I wonder if the man got his wings from the same place as the gargoyle man. Those metal feathers are so detailed, and they look really heavy.

As the angel man extends his arm, his angel lady twirling away from him, she brushes against my side.

A shock like static snaps along my skin. I look down as something wraps around my waist, but there's nothing there. I press my hand where I feel the sensation of something squeezing my stomach.

"What ...?"

A scream builds but gets caught in my throat as the invisible force tightens. I'm nearly folded in half as I'm yanked from the party, away from the lights and dancing in the smoke-shrouded street. As if in slow motion, I watch my flower crown tumble silently to the street, the little ribbons fluttering through the artificial fog as I'm thrown into absolute darkness.

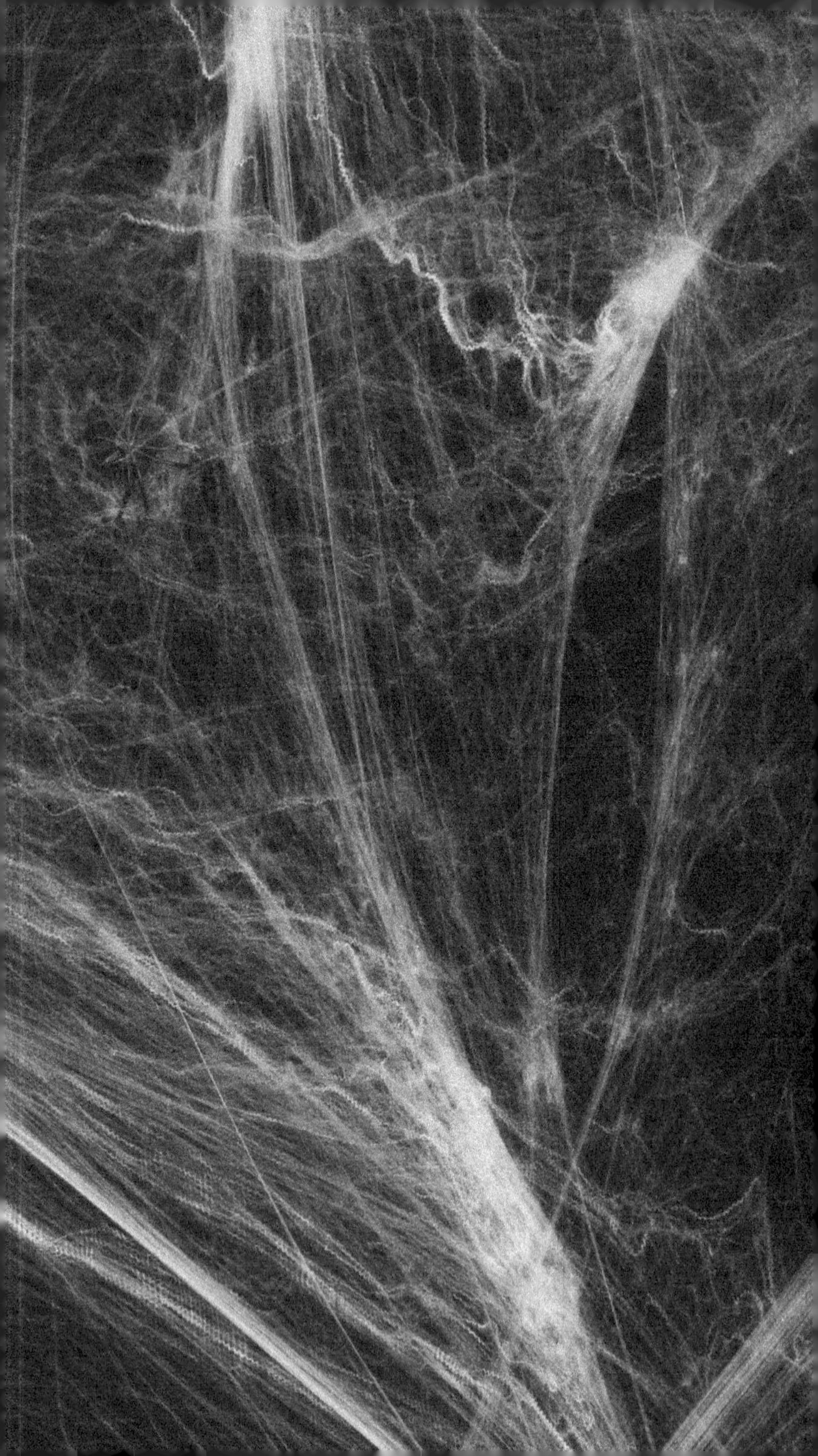

THE ANCIENT

The soft sounds of the meditation music curl around me, the deep vibrations sending soothing rhythms through my thick scaled hide, calming my soul. With every exhale, lazy smoke curls from my mouth, and the heat of my inner fire warms my belly. As I shift, the plush carpets and blankets hug my body, and I nuzzle deeper into the softness of my nest. My tail curls around me, and I sink into the nothingness of my mind. I let go. I drift.

This is the only state that maintains my sanity. I've lived too long. I've seen too much. I should end my existence ... and I almost have. Several times. But each time *something* stays my hand.

Hope.

What a cruel emotion. I don't even know what I'm hoping for.

Breath by breath, I attempt to sink deeper, tossing away thoughts as they come.

A tingle shivers down my spine.

I ignore it. After all, it *is* All Hallows' Eve in the human realm. There's always a charged quality to the atmosphere anytime the veil between realms thins and magic comes out to play. I used to love it ... The power. The freedom. The possibilities. Now, I'm just annoyed as the kinetic energy of All Hallows scratches at me, keeping me from my deep meditative state.

I take another deep breath. My tail twitches, and my claws flex involuntarily. A soft flutter tickles through the center of my being, then a gentle tug pulls at my chest. Gritting my teeth, a low growl of frustration rumbles in my chest. *What now? I just want to be left alone.*

Magic.

Like sparking electricity, power scrapes over my hide, and I crack open an eye as my growl gets louder. With a thought, the music stops, and silence presses in on my ears. I keep still, barely breathing. There's something here. In my mountain. In my home. Who or what would dare enter without my permission? No monster of this realm would be that stupid.

There's a light scraping noise and a swish of fabric. It's faint, but I have no problem picking up the sound. Both of my eyes snap open, their glow illuminating the black scales along my front legs and the faded carpets under me. Silently, I flex and press myself to my feet. My horns nearly touch the towering ceiling, and though I've tucked my wings to my sides, they press close to the walls.

Tilting my head, I listen as the soft noises pick back up. Flaring my nostrils, I inhale, dismissing the familiar scents of my home ... the gold, the jewels, the books, the fabrics, the loneliness ...

There.

Human. But how? They can't cross the veil unless

they have magic, and magic mostly died out in humans long ago. I take another deep breath. It's definitely human, and there's nothing 'other' about its scent. Nothing special. Just a boring, lost little human.

A female, by the scent of her.

My lips curl back in a wicked grin, exposing my sharp rows of teeth. Whoever this is, they are about to learn what a grave mistake they have made. Oh yes. Their fear will be a delicious precursor to their death.

And then I can go back to my solitude.

I grin as the soft sounds of her shifting reaches me. I'm in no rush. It's dark in my hoard room. Pitch dark. She won't be able to find her way out. And even if she did, there's no escape. Not from me.

I am an Ancient. One of the last four of my kind. My power is unmatched.

Lifting my giant front claw, I let a roar build in my chest.

CHAPTER 5

ANA

Fucking fuck. What the fuck happened? Where the hell am I?

I rub my throbbing hip. I'm sure there's going to be a huge bruise there from where I landed not-so-gracefully on this ... My hands pat along the hard, cold surface. It feels like a stone table.

"Or an altar."

I shiver at my whispered words ... then keep shivering, realizing how cold it is. Rubbing my arms, I try to bring some warmth to my skin, but the movement does little to alleviate the goosebumps pebbling my skin.

Widening my eyes, I lift my hand and hold it in front of my face. I can't see it even as I wiggle my fingers and bring them closer. Snapping my head back, I almost squeak in surprise as I flick myself in the nose.

"Fuck, it's dark in here. Wherever *here* is."

Biting my lip, I go back over what I remember. I was

at the party. I was dancing. That angel woman bumped into me, and then ... Tug. Darkness. But in that darkness, there was something. A ... a jewel. A black glowing jewel.

"How does a black jewel glow?" I chide myself.

My palm rubs nervously over my chest as I recall the jewel pulsing, then disintegrating. Like sparkling black sand floating on a strong wind, the particles danced before me ...

I release a gasp as I remember the black dust rushing me with a sound like a lion's roar mixed with angry storm waves crashing against rocks. It was deafening.

And then ... nothing.

So, what happened? Did I black out? Was it a dream? Am I still dreaming?

The pain in my hip tells me I'm wide awake. I draw in the air to raise my voice and call out, but then I snap my lips shut. *Don't be stupid, Ana. Just try to find a way out.*

My skirts rustle as I shift to the edge of the table. I wince as the sound seems overly loud. Slowly, I swing my feet, pointing my slippered toes, feeling for the ground. When I brush against a solid surface, I ease to my feet.

Despite the cold, my palms sweat as I grip the table behind me. I grimace as wispy spiderwebs cling to my fingers, but I refuse to let go. This hunk of slab is my only anchor in the darkness. But I need to move. Which way? Should I just stay put and wait for help? I shake my head, pushing myself forward a tiny step. Holding out my hands so I don't bust my face on anything, I shuffle forward another step, then another. As I slide my foot along the floor, my toes hit something, and a soft clinking sound reverberates around what sounds like an enormous space.

Am I in a cave?

Crouching, I pat the floor until my fingers meet something small and round. I pick it up. It's flat and has some weight to it with ridges along the edge. Gripping it in one hand, I use my other to feel around.

A pile of what sounds like hundreds of coins shifts and clatter around me. Gasping, I fall backwards, getting tangled in the diaphanous skirts of my dress. I groan when a tearing sound accompanies the continued tinkling as the small mountain of treasure settles around my feet.

"Shit. Where the hell am I? There's a pile of doubloons or some shit just sitting here? Am I in a pirate themed haunted house? Why is it so damn dark?"

Rolling over onto my hands and knees, I start to crawl, only to get caught up in my dress again. Gathering the front of my skirt, the gauzy material scratches my chest as I tuck it awkwardly into the strap of my wings. Just as my hands land back on the stone floor, ready to crawl ... a rumbling comes from everywhere all at once.

The hairs on the back of my neck raise. My fingers flex against the floor and sweat drips down my neck.

I crawl.

The rumbling gets louder.

My knee catches on the edge of my skirt, pulling it from the strap, and I pitch forward, nearly busting my nose. The ground shakes with the force of a roaring that makes my ears ring.

Nope. No. No. No.

I get my feet under me, and on trembling legs, I shuffle-run. I have no idea where I'm going, and my body tenses with the anticipation of running into a wall ... or whatever just made that noise.

Boom!

I shuffle faster.

Boom!

My toe snags on something sharp, my slipper doing nothing to protect me as a stinging pain lances up my foot.

Boom!

Something is coming. Something very, very big.

Boom!

My shoulder connects with what feels like rock. I hold back a whimper of pain as I reach out, hoping I've run into a wall that I can follow to a way out. But my fingers meet carved stone, the curves telling me it's a statue.

"Damn it. Where am I?"

Boom!

The sound is getting closer. I turn away from the statue, only for my shin to slam into something metal. Pain radiates up my leg, and I press my lips together to hold in my shout. Whatever I ran into clangs loudly as I fall. I throw my hands out to catch myself, and land in a pile of ... I don't know what. Something that feels like a rolled-up rug lays under my thighs. My stomach rests on something hard and cold, while my hands sink into another pile of coins. Or is this the same pile from before?

"Did I just run in a circle?"

I freeze, realizing how loud my whisper was in the now deafening silence. My body trembles, and I bite my lip, trying not to move, trying to be as silent as possible. The air stirs behind me, and I close my eyes against the terrifying darkness.

A hot wind blows my hair over my shoulders.

I tremble, frozen in terror as I realize it's not wind, it's breath, as a deep voice growls, "It doesn't matter how still you are, I can hear your pathetic heart racing, little human."

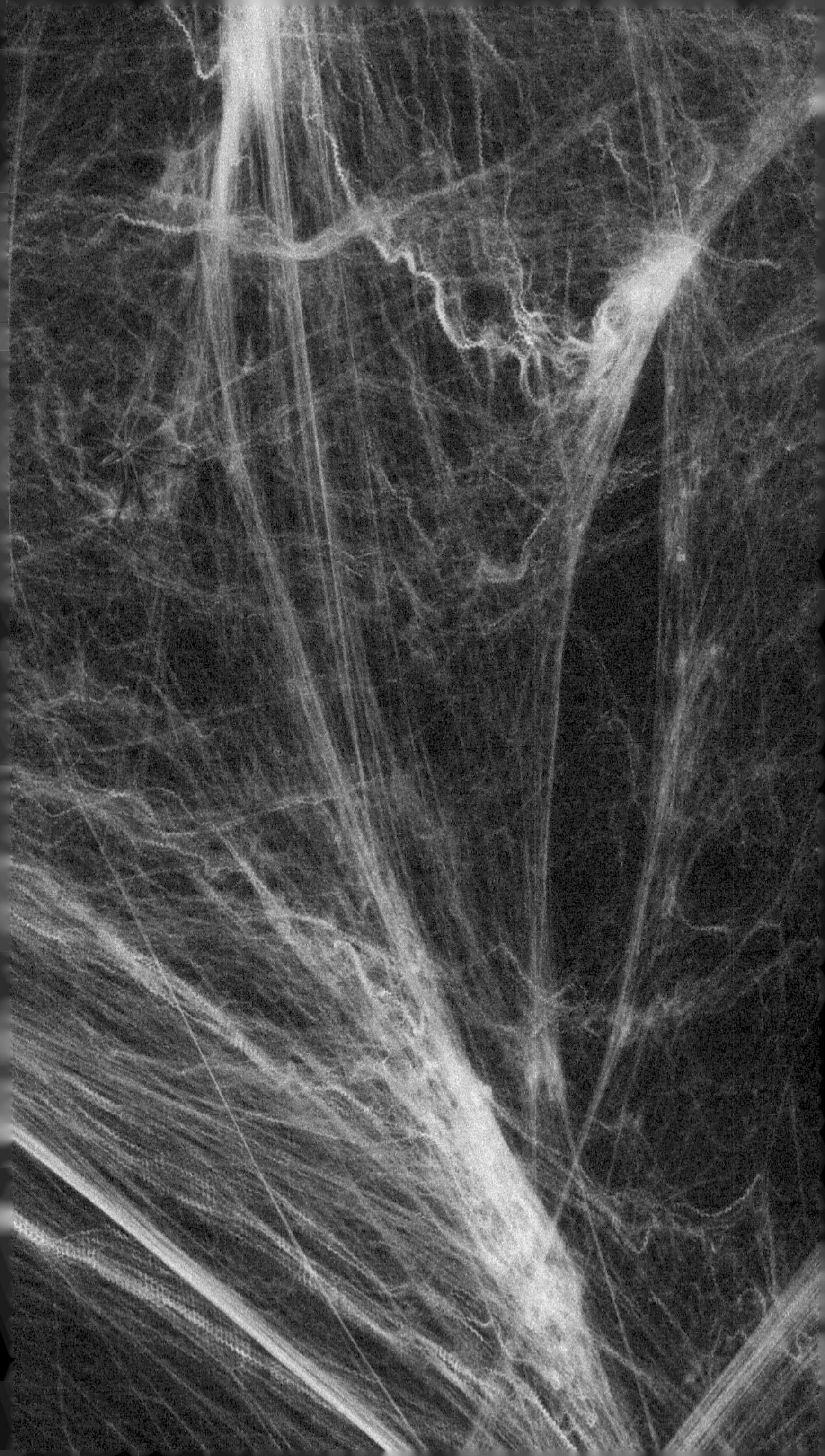

CHAPTER 6

THE ANCIENT

The female quivers where she fell into a pile of my treasures. I flick out my tongue, tasting her terror in the air. My eyes widen, and I lower my head to get closer as I slide my tongue back out.

Intriguing. Delicious. Tempting.

Crouching, I press my belly to the floor, desiring a real taste. Before I'm able to lick her, she rolls, scrambling away from me. I know she can't see in this darkness, but when she looks up, I realize the light of my eyes has revealed me to her.

Her mouth falls open, and her eyes are so wide I can see grey flecks dotting the green and brown. Beautiful.

I shake my head, not allowing myself to get distracted. I doubt she can see much of me beyond my eyes, but it's enough to have the color drain from her face.

It's a pretty face ... for a human. Delicate, with pink

lips and freckles dusting her nose and cheeks. And those eyes ... holding the tones of earth and sky. The color of her wild red hair reminds me of fresh blood staining a gold necklace. Her curls and plaits frame her shocked features. I reach out a claw, then pause, realizing I was about to caress a strand of her hair.

What the hell am I doing? Do not get distracted!

I slam my claw down in anger. The ground shakes, and a sound between a scream and a squeak punches from the little female's pretty lips. She jumps to her feet, clinging the fabric of her long skirts in one hand before she turns and runs into the darkness.

Wings? Could I have been mistaken? Is she a fairy or sprite? If so, she's rather large for either of those species and doesn't have the scent of one.

I shake my head, sending my scales rattling. It doesn't matter. She's a trespasser.

"Where are you going, little sprite?"

She keeps running, but her small size doesn't carry her far. I watch as she nears a large rack of weapons ... weapons made by humans long ago ... weapons made to kill a dragon. Too bad for them, I'm not an actual dragon.

She can't see the rack as she blindly runs from me ... or tries to. She's going to run right into it. She's going to hurt herself.

Before I know what I'm doing, I've sent my magic to illuminate the torches lining the enormous cavern, and I've wrapped my tail around her, propelling her away from the sharp weapons. She screams, clutching at my scales. As soon as I set her down, she pushes away from me and starts running again, her little feet pounding the stone floor even faster now that she can see.

So cute.

So beautiful. The flickering light of the torches makes her red curls and braids seem like they are happily dancing down her back. A flowery corset hugs her small body, her slippered feet poking out from her skirts as she sprints away from me. I notice a dark red stain on one slipper. She's hurt. She's bleeding.

The scent of her blood slams into me, and I shudder as a literal snapping sensation tightens around my heart.

Really? This little thing? She's ... my mate?

Well, this is inconvenient.

Her eyes are wide as she looks over her shoulder. "A dragon! Really? Whoever made this haunted house went way overboard. I'm suing!"

Haunted house? How rude. My home isn't haunted.

Still, her voice curls around me like a hug, and my belly glows with my inner fire. I tell myself I have no interest in this female, mate or not. I have no intention of offering my heart to anyone ... never again.

But my body moves on its own, and I lower my head until my chin rests on the ground ... *not* to get closer to her and her delicious scent. Certainly not. No. I need her to stop running before I take chase in earnest to claim what is mine.

I don't want a mate. I don't need her.

I'm appalled at how calm and soothing my voice sounds as I say, "I'm not a dragon. I'm an Ancient, which means I am far older and far more powerful than any monster in the realm."

"Well, you look like a fucking dragon!" She yells as she races away from where I've prostrated myself ... before a human. Such impudence from the little female.

As she rounds a pile of my treasures, I realize I'm smirking in amusement and quickly wipe the half-smile off my face. She slides to a stop, and her head swivels, I assume to try to find a way out.

Next to all the glitter and splendor of my hoard, I have the stray thought that she outshines everything in this room. She swallows, and I'm entranced by the movement of her throat. My gaze travels down her pale skin, appreciating the way the flowers along the top of her corset caress her small breasts ...

My entire body seizes with rage as I narrow my eyes at the familiar black magic glowing faintly from her chest.

Of-fucking-course! The fates would dare play with me like this? *She's* my mate? At least this makes my rejection of her easier.

"You." My voice drips with malice.

Her head snaps around, wide eyes on me, and she takes a trembling step backwards. Her hand presses to the swell of her small breasts, right where that foul magic seeps from her. "Me, what?"

Smoke pours from my skin, and my form shifts. I lift off my four legs as I take my bipedal form, four arms sprouting from my upper body. My tail thrashes behind me, and six horns spear up and away from my head. Dozens of eyes blink from my face and horns as I growl at her. In this body, I'm not as bulky and am slightly humanoid, but I'm even taller than before.

To her credit, her voice doesn't shake as she says, "What the fuc—"

I haul her into the air using invisible tendrils of my magic. Her screams are delightful, her hair flying behind her as I bring her right up to my face. I could swallow her with one bite. I should.

Tilting my head, I sneer at her. "So, Devana, you have finally been reborn."

The female stops thrashing. "How ... How do you know my name? No one calls me that."

My magic squeezes her until she gasps. "How do I know your name? I know your name like I know your devious mind, like I know the feel of your body under mine, like I know this innocent act is a trick, like I know your black traitorous heart."

"What? What!? What are you saying? Put me down! Let me go! I don't know what you're talking about! I ..."

Tears pool in her hazel eyes, her cheeks and nose turning red, making the soft spray of her freckles darken. Does she really not remember who she is?

No. This is a trick. An act. She is Devana. The black glow pulsing from her chest confirms it. She is the goddess of wild nature. The goddess of the forest, of the hunt, and of the moon. She was *my* goddess. My love. Until she led the human hunters to our home. Until she used her magic to bind me. Until she watched her human companions torture me. Until I killed her with my bare hands.

That was centuries ago ... never again.

The first time I met Devana was actually in Ekenys, here in the monster realm. It was during the Autumnal Equinox, and she was able to use her natural born magic as a witch to slip through The Divide. Apparently, she'd done this before, crossing into other worlds to learn, to grow and expand her power. When I came across the curvy human witch with her hands buried to the elbow in the chest cavity of a reptilian xani, I found myself intrigued.

I should have killed her.

I didn't. I fell for her.

Dismissing the memory, I glance over my shoulder, looking down at the stone slab table. The gem is gone. Just as I thought. Devana's black heart has been reborn in this human woman. She is back, just as she promised.

I roar in her face, and she scrunches her eyes closed. I wrap one of my clawed hands around her, shaking her until her teeth clatter. "Look at me, *my sweet.*" My voice drips with disgust as I use the pet name from so long ago. "Look me in the eye as I take your life. See the absolute glee on my face as I crush your black heart once more."

CHAPTER 7

ANA

I'm going to die. I don't know how I ended up here. All delusions that this is a haunted house have flown out the window. I don't know how I incurred the wrath of this monster, but it's pissed, and I'm going to die.

I must be over thirty feet in the air as it holds me in its unforgiving grip right in front of its face. It roars, and I have an unobstructed view into its wide-open mouth. Its grip tightens, and my head falls back on a gasp of pain. I swear I can feel my ribs creaking as if on the verge of breaking.

The monster's jaws snap so close to me, I feel the reverberation. A wicked grin lifts its lips. Its dozens of eyes narrow on me, fire dancing in their depths. Another of its arms lifts, and it wraps that hand around me as well. A third arm raises, a sharp claw aimed at my head.

Oh god. I can't take enough of a breath to scream.

The monster makes a noise between a growl and a

laugh as it says, "This is almost too easy, Devana, but no less than you deserve. You shouldn't have come back."

I open my mouth to tell this beast that I'm not the Devana it thinks I am, but as I do, it tosses me into its mouth. Screaming, I slide along its rolling tongue as it tries to get me between its teeth. I slam into the side of a giant fang, nearly knocking the wind out of me. My hands slip and slide, and I brace against the tooth as its tongue pushes me from behind.

I scrunch up, getting both slippered feet on the fang, just barely keeping myself out of its jaws. "I will not be eaten!" I manage to reach back without sliding between its teeth. My palm burns as I slap its tongue. I don't know if it even felt that. Nevertheless, I do it again and again as I shout, "I'm not Devana!"

I mean, I am, but not the one it believes I am ... I don't think. How could I be? But ... whatever, I need to focus on not dying.

My foot slips. My chest thumps painfully, as if something is being ripped out of me. I throw my hands up—knowing they'll do nothing to stop the monster's jaws from crushing and grinding me to bits before it swallows me down.

The shiny teeth stop a mere inch from my body. A loud coughing sound shakes my bones, and then ...

The heat of its mouth is replaced by rushing wind as the ground quickly approaches. *Did it just spit me out?* I'm relieved but a little offended. Do I taste that bad?

My hair and skirts stick to me, a thick layer of saliva coating my entire body. I flail my arms, my screams echoing off the stone walls. A second before I hit the floor, I screw my eyes shut.

Silence.

"Am I dead?"

Cracking open one eye, I dare to peek.

Both eyes pop open. I'm ... hovering. My nose is an inch from the floor, and a strange black mist swirls around me. I twist awkwardly to look over my shoulder to see if I got caught on something, though I didn't feel a tug.

Nope. Nothing. I'm just floating. Looking back down, I gasp. Waving a hand under my body, the black mist tickles my skin. "Is it ... is it coming from me?" I press my hand to my chest, and sure enough, black smoke that doesn't smell like smoke pours from my skin, swirling around my fingers before surrounding me. Waving my hand does nothing to disperse the growing cloud of mist.

What the fuck is going on?

The beast's growling voice demands my attention. "You claim you are not Devana, but your black magic protects you all the same."

I look back as the towering monster crouches. My eyes snag on his cock. Jesus fucking Christ!

Whipping my head away from the beast behind me, I swim my arms, desperate to get away. He chuckles, the sound closer now. I press my toes and fingers into the ground, trying to propel myself forward, but my spit-covered skin slips against the stone.

With a huff, I flop to the floor as the black mist suddenly dissipates.

Worry about that later. Run. Now!

Fumbling with my now soaked and heavy skirts, I get my feet under me and take off at a dead sprint. I hate running. It's the absolute worst ... until you need to run for your life. "If I survive this, I'll add more cardio into my life, I swear."

I'm jerked back, and an involuntary whimper escapes my lips, but when I look back, it's not the monster who has snagged me. My skirts mock me, hooked on the sharp edge of a metal bracket sticking out of a gods-honest trea-sure chest.

I grip the gauzy material, lamenting my ruined costume as I yank, tearing myself free.

My breath saws painfully from my lungs as I run towards a dark opening in the cavern wall. I don't know where that leads, but I just want out of here. As I sprint, my slippers pounding on the stone floor, I work one strap of my crushed wings, then the other off my shoulders, letting them fall away.

That's better.

Bunching my skirts up to my waist, I force myself to run faster. *Just a few more feet and I can slip into that tunnel. He won't fit in there.*

"Go. Faster," I command my aching legs.

He chuckles again, and I yelp at how close he sounds. *Don't look. Just run.*

I nearly dive into the tunnel, and gauze-like spider webs drift like curtains as I pass. Slapping my hand to the wall as I barrel deeper into the darkness, I don't stop until the light of the chamber behind me has completely faded.

Throwing my back against the wall, I suck air into my lungs, wiping sweat and saliva from my neck and chest. I brush my face, trying to dislodge some of the sticky webs. I don't even want to think about the possibility of spiders in my hair. Sure, I'm being chased by an angry dragon who's not a dragon, but spiders ... yuck.

After a few moments, I lift my skirts, feeling for the tears from earlier. My hands are shaking, and my legs feel like they're going to give out at any moment. I've never been this terrified, but I think adrenaline is keeping me going right now.

I must say, reading about a heroine being chased by a monster and experiencing it are wildly different. I don't like this, not one bit. Of course, when I used set my book down to press my vibrator to my clit, imagining being pursued by something dark and dangerous, my fantasies never included the monster wanting to *actually* kill me.

Still, with the one glance I got of his monster cock, I couldn't help but notice what looked like frills or ruffles along his length. I wonder what ...

No! Stop it, Ana. You're being hunted, you lunatic. Focus.

Shaking away my wayward thoughts, I find the rips in my skirts. Risking the noise—it's not like he didn't see me sprint in here—I tear the fabric all the way around, one layer after the other. Dropping the sacrificial fabric to the ground, I nod in satisfaction. My skirt now hangs in damp tatters just above my knees.

I wiggle my left foot, just now feeling the twinge of pain. I don't remember when or how I hurt it, but I can't see it in this dark tunnel, and maybe that's for the best. Planting my feet, I shove off the wall, once again pressing my hand to the rock to feel my way out.

Hot breath on my cheek makes me freeze.

He chuckles, "Did you think you had escaped me?"

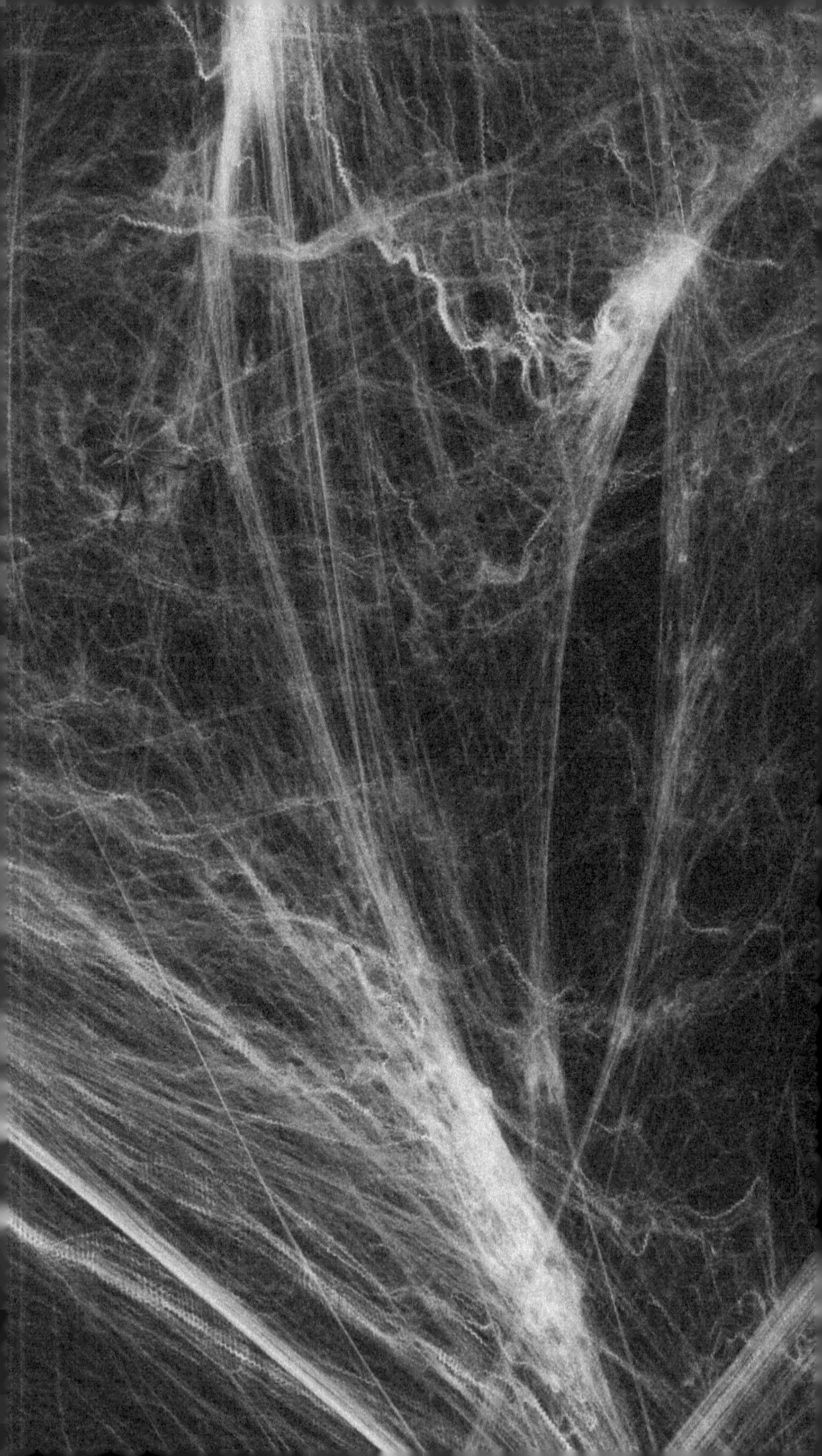

CHAPTER 8

THE ANCIENT

The taste of her rolling around in my mouth was better than ambrosia, and I've had ambrosia, so it's a fair comparison. The spirited female fought me, shouting and slapping my tongue while futilely trying to keep herself from sliding between my waiting jaws.

But when I bit down with the anticipation of crunching bones, a burst of her dark magic exploded in my mouth. It was like acid in my mouth, forcing me to spit her out.

I'm aggravated. I'm aggravated that I'm relieved. I'm also pissed.

I really fucking hate the Fates right now.

But I must say, I do like it when she runs. I like it a lot. It pulls at every primal instinct I have. Lust thrums through me, causing my cock to harden slightly. I envision chasing her until exhaustion brings her to her knees, then I'd take her until she passed out.

My cock stiffens even more as I lean in through the darkness of the tunnel to flick my long tongue up her neck. Delicious. I fight to hold back a possessive growl, because I don't want her. Certainly not.

She shrieks and takes off running once again. I lick my lips, but when I realize I'm trying to savor her taste, I clench my hands until my claws dig into my thick skin.

Fucking Fates.

I know this little female's innocence is an act, but I'm having a hard time resolving the Devana I knew with the luscious woman running away from me right now. If only she didn't look so different—red curly hair instead of straight black, green-flecked eyes instead of gold, pale freckled skin instead of warm brown, petite instead of tall and curvy—it would be so much easier to kill her if she just looked like the lying bitch I loved then hated. This little sprite reminds me of the morning sunlight from her realm. The Devana I knew was the danger hidden in the shadows.

The female's now torn and wet skirts slap around her legs, revealing tempting flashes of her thighs. No matter her appearance, that dark magic taints the air around her. I follow *my sweet* at a slow pace, letting her think she's getting away. But I hear every thud of her feet, the light scrape of her fingers over the stone walls, and the racing of her black heart.

My lips tug with a grin as I trail the long nails of each of my hands down the rock tunnel as I stroll after her. The sound is grating. Devana's breath hitches, and she picks up her pace. I may as well enjoy this little hunt for a while. I mean, what else do I have to do? She deserves every ounce of fear she's experiencing right now.

As Devana approaches a junction, I pause, curious which way she'll choose. She doesn't slow at all, and I hear her shoulder connect with the wall as she takes a hard right.

Hmm. That's the path that leads to the thermal pools ... which lead outside. Seems the hunting grounds are about to expand. Should be fun.

I follow Devana, growling every so often just so I can inhale the spicy spike of her fear. It's quite delicious.

Eventually, she slows, and her breathless voice trills down the tunnel. "I-I didn't s-steal anything, if that's what you think. And I'd b-barely count as a s-s-snack. Just"—she coughs and stumbles before picking back up into a run—"Stop this! L-leave me alone!"

Her little footfalls echo off the cavernous ceiling as she enters the thermal pool chamber, and she skids to a stop, stuttering and awed, "Oh!"

I stride into the room after her, chuckling darkly. "Ah, but you are a threat. And I have nothing but time, so keep running, *my sweet.*"

She wheezes with struggling breaths as she mumbles to herself, "Figures I'd somehow piss off a bored monster with a primal kink."

If she only knew.

She takes off running again, and a few moments later, my exceptional hearing picks up her little shout of relief as she bursts outside. I chuckle. She thinks she's free of me?

I sprout wings and take my dragon-like form once again, soaring into the skies. My gaze travels along the line of the valley until I spy the tips of the black spires of Malicious' castle. That monster likes to push his boundaries. I should have chased him away. Actually, I should have killed him for daring to make a home right on the edge of my territory, but he amuses me ... when he's not pissing me off.

Drawing my gaze back to the base of my mountain, I watch my female stumble along what amounts to little more than an animal trail.

No. Not mine!

I swoop down, the moon providing enough light to allow my shadow to cross her path. She yelps a startled scream as I say, "Run, little sprite. There's no one out here but you and me. So, run. Run. Run!"

It might be better to let the other monsters of this realm chase her down and tear her apart, saving me from having to end her myself. I have the feeling killing my mate is going to be ... painful, even without the bond solidified by my bite. I throw the thought away. Besides, there are no monsters around. None dare enter my territory. So, it's just trees and dirt and mountains for miles and miles and miles.

I spear back into the clouds, catching glimpses of her pale skin and green dress through the thick foliage far below. She runs, branches grabbing at her hair like I want to, brambles tearing at her ruined dress as if they too want to see her naked skin exposed to the moonlight.

Finally, she slows to a staggering walk. Her hands grip the bark of trees as she passes. She stumbles over a root, but manages to keep her feet. Pausing, she heaves a few deep breaths, then takes off running again.

I lick my muzzle as I circle over her. She has spirit. What will it take to break her? A tiny voice in my head says, *Your mate doesn't deserve this*. I growl, talking back to myself. "Devana does. Fuck the Fates."

The possessive urges are riding me hard. They have been ever since I first saw her. But now, the protective mate instincts tug at my heart, telling me to wrap her in my arms and ... care for her.

No.

After ten minutes, she once again slows to a walk, then stops. She bends over, panting with hands on knees.

That won't do.

I swoop down, changing my form to that of a hellhound. I growl, stalking her from the shadows of the forest. I know the moment she sees my glowing eyes, because her lips drop open in a perfect "o" that makes me want to lick her, then sink my claiming bite into her neck.

No. Focus.

My growl gets louder, and the scent of her fear permeates the air. But when she doesn't move, I release a bark, and that gets her going. She takes off, branches breaking and leaves crunching in her haste to get away from me.

The hunt continues.

I pace her, snarling from her right, snapping my jaws from her left, brushing my fur against her calf. I herd her through the woods of my valley until we have spent several hours weaving back towards my mountain home.

I've given her a few chances to rest and catch her breath, making her believe she lost me ... all while I watched, scenting her, craving her. And staunchly ignoring the persistent fluttering in my chest.

A deep growl rumbles within me. I can't let myself get lost in the chase. Or to get lost in her. It doesn't matter how long she runs, how far she goes. In the end, I'll rip out her heart. Only this time, I will destroy it completely.

The painful throb in my chest makes me angry. Suddenly, this hunt has lost its appeal.

With a thought, I slice through the space in front of Devana's path. She doesn't notice, running right through the portal. My magic wraps around me, taking me back to the thermal pools inside my mountain.

Devana slams into me, her face smacking into my

stomach ... close to my cock, but not close enough. On impulse, my form swells, making me taller, and my half-hard length rubs against her chin, the frills fluttering as if reaching for her.

I laugh as she stumbles back, her wide eyes fixed on my cock. The steam curling up from the pools wraps around us, making the moment feel more intimate. I make my body smaller as I step closer to her, but she still needs to crane her head back to look at my face. The face of a monster. The face of her killer.

The face of her mate, though she doesn't know that. And she never will.

My shadow overtakes her, and I reach out a hand, claws extended as I say, "You cannot escape me, Devana. I will kill you a thousand times for what you did."

The fear on her face melts away, replaced by glorious rage.

Ah, that's a bit closer to the Devana I know and hate.

With hands on hips, she actually glares at me. "Look! I am not who you think I am. Yes, my name is Devana, but—"

"Don't give me your excuses. I've fallen for your lies in the past, and I won't do it again."

A bead of sweat gathers in the hollow of her throat and lazily descends between her breasts. I blink, gritting my teeth together. I will not be entranced by this witch again! I won't! Mate bond be damned!

Fuck the Fates.

With a growl, I grow five feet, spearing my tail towards her stomach, ready to gut her. Her eyes go wide. My heart sinks with dread, even as my skin prickles with the anticipation of her death. It's a dizzying dichotomy, and I feel myself holding back.

I've been holding back since she appeared. For what?

Sentiment? For some misplaced feelings of love that won't fade no matter how hard I try?

With a growl, I put more force into my killing blow.

Black light explodes from her chest, tossing me into the air. As I tumble backwards, I almost laugh. She surprised me. When was the last time I was caught off guard?

I hit the wall, easily landing on my feet as I recall ... the last time I was truly shocked was when Devana betrayed me all those years ago.

Looking across the room, I catch the flutter of her ruined skirts through the mist as she runs back towards the tunnel that leads outside. We could do this all again. And again, until she breaks. But I'm stalling. I need to end this.

With a casual burst of speed, I silently come up behind her, drinking in her racing heart and panting breaths. I smirk as I flick a hand, ripping open another portal in front of her. As I step through behind her, my clawed feet sink into the worn threads of the old rug.

Why did I bring her here?

With an "oomph," Devana barrels into the arm of the velvet chair sitting in front of my bed chamber's cold fireplace. Her face slams into the seat cushion, and her legs fling up with an impressive arch of her back. One of her little slippers flies off, smacking the wall before falling to the floor.

I bite my lips to keep from bursting into the laughter that's shaking my shoulders.

With her momentum fully stopped, her legs flop back down, her toes brushing the carpet, leaving her tattered skirts up around her waist.

Fuck me.

I'm not laughing anymore. Her perfect ass presents itself to me, a thin thread between her cheeks, the silky fabric doing little to hide her delicious cunt from me.

I realize all four of my hands are hovering over her creamy skin. When did I move closer? With a growl, I grab her waist, lifting and turning her. She winces, and tears pool in her hazel eyes as one of my claws digs into her side, so I loosen my grip.

What the fuck am I doing? Just kill her already.

The stone walls echo my progress across the room as I step off the worn rug and my claws click on the bare floor. Her tiny fingers try to pry my hands away from her body as she pleads, "Please. I'm not he—"

Slapping one hand over her mouth, I use two others to grip the midnight-blue curtains, yanking with a little too much force. Moonlight streams into the room through the massive double doors, a few glass panes chipped and broken from the years of neglect. I don't bother to look around, knowing what I'd see: dusty memories I locked away long ago. A room made for *her*, but never used because she hated the monster realm and my monster form. And it turns out, she hated me.

I grip the iron handles, throwing open the doors and stepping onto the balcony carved into the side of my mountain. The claws of two of my hands dig deep grooves into the stone balustrade as I brace myself and lean over into the eternal night of the monster realm.

The valley spreads before me, and I'm embraced by the shadow of the towering peaks of the mountain range rising behind me. It's a calm night, the dark trees standing still without a breeze to sway their branches.

I look down at the female in my grip. She has gone still. Her nose flares above where my fingers dig into her face as she tries to suck in air. Tears glitter in her eyes, but don't fall.

She's so beautiful—so different from my Devana, but that black heart beats within her chest all the same.

Never again.

I toss my mate over the railing, and a piece of my heart goes with her. Good riddance to both.

Her wide eyes hold mine as she seems to hang suspended for a long moment, her skirts flapping around her, her damp curls dancing around her face.

Then she falls with a piercing scream.

I turn away, trying to ignore the agony in my heart. Crossing back into my bed chamber, I tell myself I'm not affected by Devana's screams filling the valley behind me. My shoulders bunch. I use my magic to create long, silvery hair that cascades between my horns and down my back, just so I can pull on it.

She's still fucking screaming. Still falling.

I throw my head back and roar, ripping some of my hair out. The slight pain feels good. I bite my lip until I taste blood. Dropping my arms, I sigh, flopping backwards onto the large bed. Dust billows around me, and I wrinkle my nose. My claws dig into the bedding as I wait for the abrupt end to her screams to tell me she's struck the ground.

Any moment now.

One of my hands lands on my chest, trying to hold in the hurt. I'm physically trembling with the need to save her. She's min—NO!

Devana's screams erupt into the room as a swirling black portal—one I most certainly did *not* create—opens right above me. I'm so shocked, I barely manage to use my magic to slow her descent so she doesn't splat against me. What a mess that would make.

Devana lands on my chest, and all my arms wrap around her, holding her small body to mine.

And now this luscious, traitorous bitch is in my bed.

Well, fuck.

ANA

I'm no longer falling.

And I'm not dead.

I whisper, "Run, Ana."

Dust clings to my throat, and my voice cracks from my earlier screams. When I shift to move, something restricts my movements. Arms? Tilting up my chin, I stare into a dark face and glowing eyes. What? Are we ...? Are we on a bed? An enormous bed. The hard muscles beneath me flex. He's so warm. And those ruffles I saw ...

Wait, what? No! Focus, Ana.

Clenching my fists, I push against his chest, and it rumbles with a sound close to a purr. A violent purr. Despite that, I have the absurd urge to relax into him. His voice whispers over my hair, giving me goosebumps. "Welcome back, Devana. Seems killing you is going to be a bit harder than I thought. Should be fun."

"I'm not the FUCKING Devana you think I am!" I

squirm, kicking and pushing against him. Surprisingly, he lets me go, and I roll to the edge of the bed. As soon as my feet hit the ground, I run towards the first door I see. My sweaty hands slip on the handle, but I manage to twist it and yank open the thick wood door. I don't give myself a chance to stop and think as I sprint down the hall to my left.

Away. I need to get away.

Another door looms before me, and I wipe off my hand in preparation.

My thighs collide with the edge of the mattress, but I'm able to catch myself this time before I tumble heels-over-ass. What the fuck is happening? I keep ... slipping from one place to another?

Pushing away from the bed and his grinning face, I sprint back out the door, turning right this time. My lungs are on fire, the cut on my foot burns, and at some point, I lost one of my slippers. There's a stitch in my side that threatens to double me over, and my ribs still ache from where that monster nearly crushed me earlier.

But I run. Because what choice do I have? It's either run or die.

I'm exhausted. The thought of taking another step nearly overwhelms me. I swallow my tears. I don't have time to cry, and I certainly don't have the breath to cry. Later. I'll break down later.

First. Survive.

I pass a few closed doors and pick one randomly, wrenching it open. I step through, and ...

"Damn it!" I'm in the same bedroom. "What the fuck?"

A chuckle from the bed draws my gaze back to him. He's now propped up against the massive headboard, two arms crossed behind his head, two arms resting on his stomach ... his lickable stomach.

Mentally, I slap myself. I need to ease up on the monster romance books.

His dozens of glowing red eyes blink at me, some crinkled with the lines of his grin. He looks much too pleased with himself, with his legs crossed at the ankles.

As if I amuse him.

Bastard.

A burst of heat and light erupts behind me. I spin, my heart racing, but it's only a fire in the giant stone fireplace lending its warmth to this frigid place. I frown. Something's off. It's silent. There's no wood, no crackling sounds, so I assume it's a magical fire.

I have the crazy urge to go over and touch the flames to see if they burn, but I turn back around, unwilling to give this beast my back for longer than a moment. He is smaller than he was before, but still huge with miles of that dark skin, the horns, the tail, the multiple arms ... and now a beautiful mane of silver hair tumbles between his horns and over his shoulders.

I clench my fists, ignoring how my breath hitches as my gaze wanders down his defined torso. I stop before I hit the v of his hips. No reason to go *there*.

With slow, sliding steps, I back away towards where I know the door to be, and he just watches. The second I cross the threshold, I turn and sprint ... across the floor of the bedroom and right into the waiting claws of the grinning monster who is now sitting on the edge of the bed.

His fingers wrap all the way around my neck and squeeze, pulling me between his thighs. "I told you, there is no running from me, Devana."

With barely any effort at all, he lifts me off my feet. I kick at him, panting with the pain of my neck being stretched and my airway being restricted. He's only using one of his four hands to hold me up, the other three casually resting on the bedding. I feel like an insect dangling from his claws.

Little white stars dance at the edges of my vision, and I sputter. "I ... I'm n-not her."

A pulse flutters in my chest, and I think it's my heart struggling to beat, but then a burst of black light spears from my body, hitting the monster right in the face.

He drops me with a bellow that hurts my ears. I'm too dazed to catch myself, and I fall to my knees, clutching my throat as I cough and gasp. Oxygen. Sweet, sweet air.

When I look up, I'm met with an eyeful of his fancy cock. Yup, confirmed. His cock has frills or ruffles or ... I'm not sure what to call them. As I stare, they stiffen and flutter like they're waving hello to me, and my mouth drops open.

His growl snaps me out of my stupor, and I fall back on my ass, scooting away from the intense look in the many eyes glaring down at me. He leans forward, his cock growing even larger.

I yelp, "Holy shit!"

I flip onto my hands and knees, getting my feet under me, but before I can kick into a run, a hand wraps around my neck, hauling me off the ground once more.

He stands, and my back slams into his chest. His breath tickles my ear. "With the same breath you use to tell me you are not my Devana, you blast me with your foul magic."

I'm about to scream once again that I AM NOT HIS DEVANA, but that pressure grows in my chest again. Before I can brace for it, another pulse of something—magic?—explodes from me. I'm ripped from his grip, and I fly across the room. Cat reflexes I do not have, so I land hard on my side with a grunt. My body slides across the floor until I slam into the far wall, my head smacking against the rock surface. Pain. Nausea. My skull feels too small for my brain. I see two of him for a second before my vision clears. I'm tempted to just close my eyes and give in, but I want to live. I *will* survive this ... somehow.

He stalks towards me, and flames flicker to life along his skin.

Is he burning? No. I'm not that lucky. Nope, my luck has me facing an angry monster who's determined to kill me ... and now is magically on fire. Great. Just great.

His tail lashes angrily, but with every stride he takes, that strange pressure builds in my chest that I now know precedes the black mist. I meet his eyes, the pair centered between his largest horns, and I'm captured in his gaze. I brace my hands on the floor to stave off the feeling of falling into him. An absurd urge tingles along my finger-tips ... the urge to crawl *towards* him, not away. There's rage in his eyes, yes, but there's also pain and sorrow.

He hates her, his Devana.

And he thinks I'm her.

Tears prick my eyes. My chest feels too tight. I'm on the verge of releasing a full-blown sob, and I don't know why the thought of him hating me hurts so much.

I'm just exhausted. Yes, that's it. I'm delirious and not thinking straight, obviously.

He stops, towering over my prone body, all arms bent with hands on his hips. A wicked smile reveals his sharp teeth, and the fire licking along his skin flares brighter as he says, "Your black magic protects you from my physical attack, but I have nothing but time, Devana. I *will* kill you. Fates be damned."

Fate? What?

I press myself to sit up with my back against the wall,

unable to hold back a wince at the throbbing pain pulsing from the back of my head. His body shimmers, going blurry for a second before he changes. Bones protrude from his skin, and his head turns skeletal like a wolf's. Fire burns in the empty sockets of his eyes and behind the exposed bones of his ribs. He roars, the heat drying my eyes, and I gag at the stench of burnt hair. Frantically, I pat out the red embers eating at my curls.

With a bellow, he breathes liquid fire that streams from his boney jaws. I throw up my arms, covering my face. After a moment, I peek between my forearms. It's hot, but I'm not burning. That swirling black mist curls from my chest, surrounding me, keeping the magma-like substance at bay.

The flames melt away, but before I'm able to catch my breath in relief, he lunges at me. An involuntary scream bursts from my lips as he slams into the barrier of mist. Backing away, the monster shakes his head like a dog that just ran into a wall. I'd laugh if I wasn't so terrified.

Like a caged animal, he prowls, lips pulled back with his low growls, saliva dripping from his fangs. His eyes burn red as he inspects the shadowy shield around me. When those rage-filled eyes meet mine, I'm filled with despair. He really hates his Devana. He hates *me*. I feel like I'm breaking. My heart aches. I'm frustrated. I'm angry. I'm sad. I don't understand anything that's happening.

I need to do something to keep these overwhelming emotions from taking over, so I scoot up the wall, bracing myself to keep my shaking knees from buckling. Side-stepping towards the balcony door, I aim for some kind of freedom. He follows, stalking, vicious growls shaking the room. I feel the sound throughout every inch of my body, and goosebumps cover my flesh.

Keep moving, Ana.

Just as I reach the doors, the beast backs away, rising on his hind legs, shifting his form once more. He melts into a gooey, bubbling puddle on the floor at my feet, then a geyser of black liquid sprays into the air. The droplets turn into insects. Their buzz gets louder, and my heart rate picks up. Little back bodies fill the room, swarming around me. They cover the walls, the windows, the doors, until a sea of insects overtakes my vision. They don't get past the mist still surrounding me, but my panic is in full swing.

I'm going to choke on them! They're going to get inside me, in my lungs, under my skin. "No. No. No."

A satisfied hum echoes around the room, and the bugs fall to the floor, gathering in the center of the room before rising and coalescing into his humanoid shape, his horns scraping the ceiling, his tail swishing lazily behind him.

He says, "I don't know why you're continuing to pretend to be"—he waves a hand at me—"this. I know you, Devana. I know your power. Face me as you truly are. Stop trying to gain an advantage with this innocent act. It won't work."

I'm too exhausted and confused to come up with a response. He tilts his head at me, frowning as he says, "Fine. Cling to this cheep trick. It doesn't matter. I've sealed this room. Not even your black magic can break through." He turns, crosses the room, resting his large hand on the door handle. All I do is stand still and blink after him. He pauses, looking over his shoulder. "You're trapped, Devana. There is no escape. You're *mine*."

Something possessive rumbles in those words before he ducks through the door and softly closes it behind him.

He just ... he just left? Is this a trick?

I turn, gripping the balcony door handles. They won't

budge. I shake them. Nothing. Bracing my feet, I pull with my whole body. The doors don't even groan. Careful to avoid the sharp edges, I reach for a broken pane of glass. My fingers brush against an invisible barrier. The outside night air cools my skin, but I can't push my hand through.

"Damn it!"

I stomp to the door leading to the hall. Once again, the handle doesn't move, and it remains firmly shut. Turning, I lean my back against the door, looking around the room, then I press a hand to my chest, looking down at my ruined dress. "Where's the magic now? Care to blast open these doors?"

I wait, but nothing happens. No buildup of pressure, no black mist. Seems his Devana, whoever she is, only reacts when the big bad is around.

I traverse the room ... twice ... trying to find a way out. At least the magical fire is still blazing in the fireplace, though its silence is unnerving. With no wood, the soothing crackling is absent, and it freaks me out. But I welcome the heat, because I'm cold. And I'm exhausted, and afraid, and pissed, and ... alone.

My body is so heavy, I nearly topple over as I lean down, taking my remaining slipper off. The silk is dirty and stiff against my fingers as I let it fall to the floor. I trudge towards the bed, swaying as the adrenaline quickly leaves my body. I'm crashing. Hard. I shouldn't let my guard down. I for sure shouldn't sleep. But rest will do me good, right? Help me fight another day? Or at least another few hours?

I'm covered in sweat and dirt and dried saliva. I stink. I would kill for a relaxing dip in those pools I ran past earlier. I recall how steam curled up from their surfaces, making me believe they would be deliciously hot. But I'm trapped in this room, and I'm just so tired.

I flip the bedding back, and an accompanying plume of dust swirls into the air. I cough, waving my hand before my face before flopping onto the mattress and curling into one of the many pillows. Hugging one to my chest, I pull the blankets over me, ignoring the musty smell.

This is nothing like my books. No fancy dick is worth this.

I huff a little laugh, but that opens the floodgates. My tears fall on a choked sob. My throat burns, and my ribs feel like they're scraping against my skin. I cry into the pillows until I'm hiccupping, and snot drips from my nose. I can't stop. There's too much built up inside, and it's all rushing out. The tears keep coming, and I scream into the blankets.

Exhaustion finally wins, and as I sink deeper into the comfort of the bed, I slip into dreams where all too familiar eyes smile down at me. I know they should be red and glowing, but instead they are a soft, ice blue. A chiseled jaw with a dusting of a blond beard highlights his all-too human face. I don't know how I know it's the monster, but I do. Intricate plaits hold back his blond hair, and clothing made of leather and fur covers his body ... still impressively muscled even in this human body. He caresses my cheek, calling me *his sweet*. His touch is so tender, I can't reconcile it with the monster I know him to be.

The dream shifts, and his laughter fills the crisp air around us as brown and orange leaves fall to the forest path we're walking down. He holds my hand, and my fingers interlace with his, but there's something burning in my chest. Impatience. Hunger. Anger. What I'm feeling is so at odds with my soft smile, it makes me dizzy.

It hits me—I'm acting in love while a deep hatred churns in my heart. But why?

The scene changes again. Pleasure. So much pleasure. My toes curl as he thrusts into me, his blue eyes holding the faintest glow of red in their centers. He growls, and I clench around him, but my hand snaps out, wrapping around the front of his throat. That black mist stings his skin in admonishment for letting his monster show. My long nails dig into his flesh, and I tsk. His movements slow down, and the little glowing embers in his eyes die.

As if these memories are my own, I know he hates wearing this human form, and the fact that he hides the monster to look human for me makes me ... happy? He'd do anything for me. He is mine to do with as I please, and it delights me.

I shake my head. No. This is wrong. I want to sit up and demand he give me more, that he gives me all of him, the eyes, the growls, the claws, the horns, the tail, the frills. Gods, the frills. But this dream doesn't allow me any control.

He kisses my neck, hands caressing my breasts—breasts that are much larger in this dream world—as he rocks into me. I'm close, clenching around him every time he sinks deep inside me. I know he's close too, but I dig my nails into his flesh until angry red marks appear. He reaches between us, using his thumb to circle my clit, and oh my god! He grunts as blood drips down his neck from where my nails have punctured him. His thumb circles faster and with more pressure as he says, "Come for me, my sweet. Please."

The intrusive thought floats through my mind that I don't care if he comes. In fact, I prefer he didn't. It keeps him on a tighter leash.

I have a moment to be disgusted with myself before sparking pleasure erupts from my center, rolling through me like shock waves. Even my fingertips are tingling.

The scene shifts again.

I'm standing in the same bedroom, but it's dark now, and there's a maliciousness to the shadows. Crickets chirp outside, and his soft breaths come from the bed I'm standing next to. His broad chest still has a slight sheen of sweat to it. His cock tents the blanket, and I smirk. Poor big, bad monster didn't get to come because *I* said so. My hands curl into fists as I stare down at him, craving ... I want his magic. I want his power. He possesses so much, and with All Hallow's Eve coming in a few days, I'll seize the moment. I'll take what I want, what I deserve. I've earned it by taking this monster to my bed.

I don't like this dream. I feel it turning into a nightmare. I want to wake up.

Another shift in the dream, and I'm outside. Cloaked figures surround me as we stride with purpose, following the worn path towards my cottage. Mine. Not ours. Soon, he will be dead, and my powers will be unmatched. My magic curls around me, dark and crackling. His love blinds him to my intentions. He doesn't even feel the binding I slip over him as he steps out of the cottage into the night. His gaze travels over the torches held aloft by those I've recruited—anyone with even a touch of magic to help me hold this creature while I strip him of every ounce of power he has.

When his eyes meet mine, he looks positively confused. Stupid male.

This bitch is the worst! I don't like this! Wake up, Ana!

The dream holds me captive as I lift my hand, shocked to see it bloodied with a symbol carved into my flesh. A ring falls from my fingers, thudding softly on the dirt. It's a near-silent sound, but it feels like a nail being hammered into a coffin.

As magic spears from my chest towards the monster who gave me his love, I try to shout a warning. He doesn't deserve this. But all that comes out is a cackling laugh that is not my own as my power slams into his body, siphoning his magic into me.

I try to back up, becoming more and more certain that this isn't some random dream. *This is a memory. This is the Devana the monster thinks I am.*

The witches around me tighten their formation, lashing their magic against him. He bellows into the night. I know he's holding back because he thinks he loves me, and that's why I'll win. I'll have everything, and he will die ... for love.

That knowledge delights Devana. But I'm disgusted with myself for thinking like that ... even knowing it's not really me ... right?

A cloaked witch to the monster's left plunges a dagger into his side. He growls, but my binding holds. A slash tears through the flesh of his back. Another rips across the back of his leg, and he falls to his knees. My magic continues to suck his power from him, and it pours into me. I feel high. I feel my sanity slipping.

How do I stop this?

It's a memory. There's no stopping what has already happened.

He groans, tucking his head, gripping his chest where my magic connects us as he whispers, "Why?"

I laugh. I'm crazy. I'm drunk on magic. I'm going to kill him.

The crazed laughter coming from my lips cuts off as he breaks my binding as easily as snapping a single thread. The witches fall to the ground, blood pouring from their eyes, ears, and noses. They choke and writhe, and then go still. Dead. All of them dead. That fast. He's still that strong.

Devana pauses with the first lick of fear I've felt from her.

Yes!

In the dream, I flick my wrist as Devana tries to put up a shield, but even with the amount of magic she stole from him, I'm too slow. There's a punch of pain, and when I look down, my heart is outside my body, still thumping in his bloodied, clawed hand. His skin turns dark, and his eyes burn red as horns spear out of his head.

The monster is unleashed.

Fear grows into horror as I watch my own heart's blood drip between his claws.

And I'm relieved.

I ... No, Divana manages to send the last tendrils of her magic into her sputtering heart, turning it into a black jewel. She spits up blood, and I feel it coat my throat as she growls, "I'll be back."

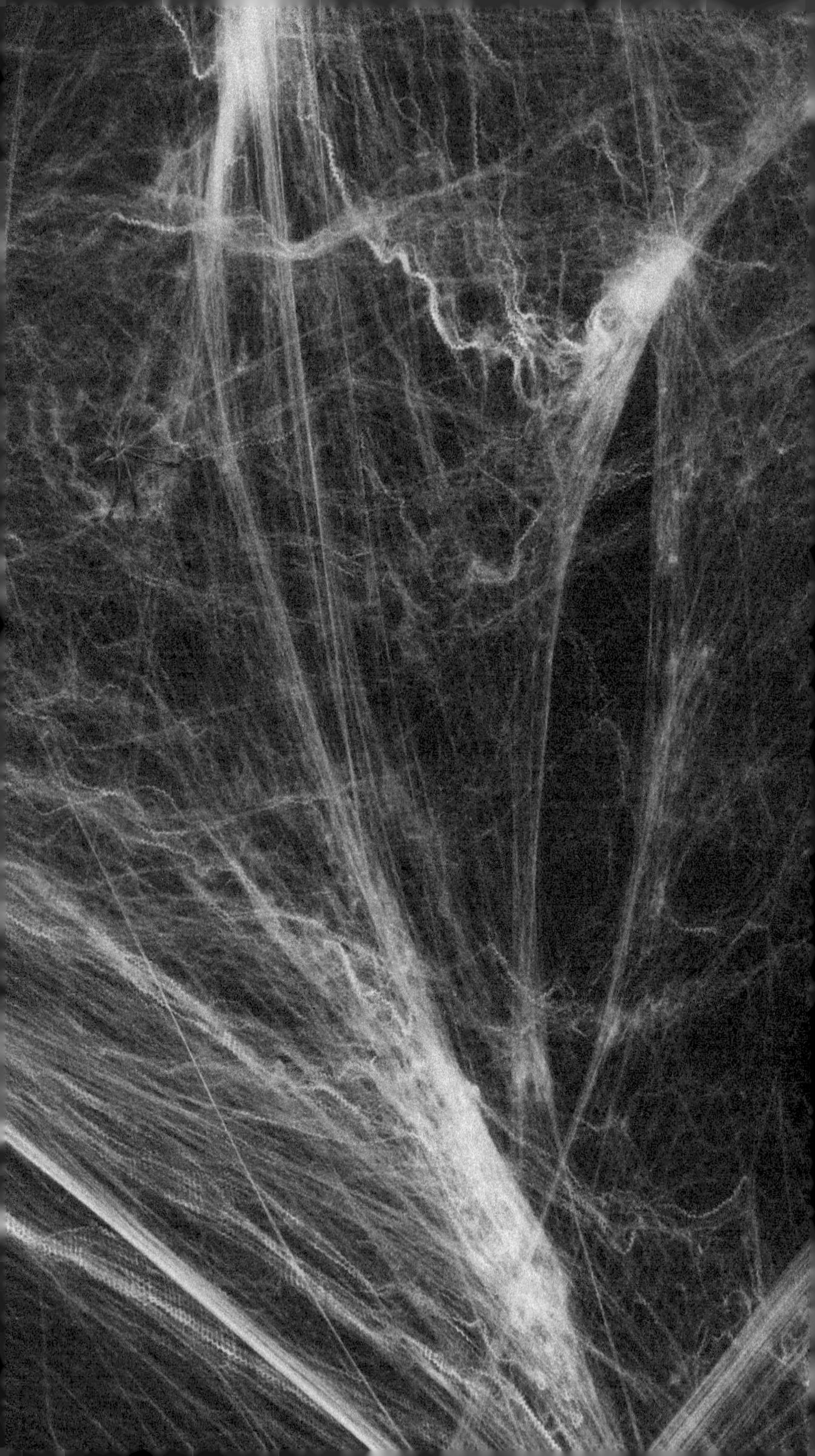

CHAPTER 10

THE ANCIENT

My claws dig grooves into the wall outside my bedroom as I listen to Devana weeping.

Why? What have I done to anger the Fates so? My chest hurts. My legs ache with the need to go to her. I grit my teeth, punching my claws deeper into the wall. It's just the mate bond. I'm stronger than some fated shackle.

From within the room, Devana hiccups, coughing on a sob. Her muffled scream tears through my heart. I look down when the door handle creaks under my grip. I don't remember moving. Okay, maybe I'm not as strong as I thought.

Enough of this! Why torture myself?

I storm down the hall, flicking open a portal to the main chamber deep in the caves. I call up the meditation music, making it loud enough that the resonance sends little pebbles on the ground hopping and bouncing. Taking my dragon form, I curl into my nest, turning first one way, then another, trying to settle. My tail twitches as her softening cries still reach me. This isn't like Devana at all. She doesn't cry unless someone is watching and she has something to gain from their sympathy. So why ...

Fuck!

I stand with a growl and leap through the vent hole in the ceiling. Spreading my wings to the night sky, I soar over my mountain. Higher and higher. I can't shake the memory of the little female landing on my chest in my bed. The way her body molded to mine. The way my arms held her tight.

My mouth waters.

I'm in trouble here.

The first time I met her all those years ago, Devana wasn't my mate, but I loved her ... didn't I? Was it love? It doesn't matter now. I can't allow her to live. I don't care who she's pretending to be. Her innocent act won't work. I know her. She'll keep coming back to kill me and steal my magic. She'll never succeed, but ...

I'm tangled in my feelings. She's mine. I hate her. I want her. I need to kill her.

I can't.

More like you won't.

I growl at myself as the moonlight glimmers along my scales. The power of All Hallows Eve has waxed, peaked, and is now waning. Perhaps, without the aid of the additional magic of this night, Devana's own powers will decrease, making it easier to destroy her.

Excuses, excuses. Even at her strongest, you're more powerful. You're still stalling.

I make a few lazy circles over my mountain, scowling. A tiny, weeping human female has chased me from my own home. Still, I don't return, because if I'm honest with myself, I must admit I'm not strong enough to listen to her sorrow and not try to comfort her.

Once again, I entertain the thought of taking her outside my territory to let the other monsters of this realm do the job for me.

I know I won't.

I fly, pulling up every memory of that fateful night ... of the night those witches came down the path to our little cottage. The torches in their hands made their faces look inhuman—they certainly had the bloodlust of a monster. I could have wiped them out with a single flick of my hand, but Devana stood there in their midst. Her smiling eyes held mine as she raised her bloody hand, showing me the rune carved into her flesh. I force myself to remember that pulse of pain in my heart the moment I realized she had bound me and my magic using that token of my love—a ring I forged for her from the depths of my mountain. But it was my affection for her more than that bloody sigil that held me in place as her magic attacked me. She brought me to my knees right in front of our cottage where we had made so many happy memories.

At least I thought we were happy. I left my realm for her. I tolerated a human form for her. I gave her pleasure, sometimes at the expense of my own.

Never again.

Familiar rage swirls through me, and I growl to the stars. Yes. Yes, this is better. Anger is better than sorrow. I can do something with anger.

I fly through the remainder of the turn—what the humans would call a day, but we don't have sunlight here, only the turning of the stars in the sky. As the new turn begins, I spear back towards my mountain with renewed determination to kill Devana and be done with her forever ... like I should have done all those centuries ago.

Shifting my form as I land on my balcony, I flick my magic, opening the ruined doors. I stride inside then stop.

My mate is sleeping in my bed, and again, I'm struck with how different she looks from the Devana I knew. Her red hair, though tangled and matted, calls to my fingers to see if it's as soft as it looks. Her freckled cheeks are red, and her eyes are swollen from her tears. Soft breaths escape her parted lips, and I swallow the urge to kiss that mouth until she wakes.

I shake my head and stalk to my bed.

Faster than a human eye can track, I snap an arm out and wrap my hand around her throat. Her eyes fly open, but she's unable to make a sound past my tight grip. Her little fingers claw at my hand, trying to find the space to take a breath.

I laugh to hide my sorrow at causing my mate pain as I pull her to my face.

Fuck, she smells good. Beneath the sweat and dirt, my dried saliva covers her skin, marking her as mine. There's also a scent that I instinctually recognize as hers, apples and honey. Delicious.

No!

My lips brush hers as I whisper, "Let's try this again."

CHAPTER 11

ANA

The monster squeezes, and there's nothing I can do to keep my body from going lax. I shift, trying to create space to breathe, only to realize my pussy is wet and aching from the orgasm he gave me in that dream.

Damn.

I'm losing consciousness ... at least I'm no longer in the nightmare ... Devana was an awful person ... I understand the hatred he has for me. I hate her now too, but ... how—I bite the inside of my cheek to keep from passing out—how do I make him see *me*, and not his Devana?

The balcony doors stand open behind him. My vision blurs then sharpens. It's still dark out. Is it the same night? Did I sleep through an entire day? Or multiple days? How long have I been here? I may have slept, but exhaustion still pulls at my body.

His deep voice pulls me from my spinning thoughts. "Have you given up already, Devana?"

He chuckles, and I suck in air as he disappears. I have a mere moment to be grateful at being able to breathe before a giant spider-like creature appears. The segments of its back end glisten, its many legs clicking on the floor. But the front of its body is grotesquely humanoid. There's a greyish torso rising from the spider's segments with long stringy hair clinging to a balding head with white eyes. It grins at me, showing off its serrated teeth, and with a screech, its body rumbles.

My feet scramble in the tangle of blankets as hundreds of fist-sized spiders burst from its main body. The creatures skitter and scrape all around the room, flooding the space with the shrill sound of their legs clacking against stone. It's deafening, and so terrifying my body shuts down. I can't move. I barely breathe. I'm sweating and shivering. I can't take this.

They rush towards me, and I close my eyes.

"Uh uh uh." My eyes fly open at the closeness of his voice. He's back in his usual form, and at this point I find the familiarity reassuring. His nose is an inch from mine, that terrifying smile on his face. "Eyes on me, *my sweet*."

His voice is pure sin, but that's what he called her in the dream. I hate it. *Don't call me that! Anything but that.*

His tongue flicks out, tasting my cheek with a long, slow lick. He emits a sound that reminds me of a kitten purring ... Well, okay, maybe a lion purring. *Do lions purr? Doesn't matter.*

He grows and expands, filling the space until he's all I see as he hunches over me. His silver hair tickles my upturned face. I raise my arms in defense as he wraps one gigantic hand around me. He's so large, his grip squeezes me from chest to mid-thigh.

I've been in his hold before, but this time is different. There's a coldness to his gaze, a resignation. As he tightens his fist, fire erupts along his fingers. The flames burn my dress, then my skin. I scream, then whimper in agony before screaming again. Tears stream down my cheeks. It hurts. I gag on the smell of my own burnt flesh.

Where did the black mist go?

I'm so tired. Tired of being afraid. Tired of being in pain. But memories of my dream come back, and I cling to the hate I feel for Devana and what she did to him. I raise my arms, spreading them wide to place my hands on either side of his massive jaw. His skin is rough, but pleasant under my palms. He growls again, his lips peeling back to show his teeth. The pain makes my vision go blurry again, but I focus on him.

I stroke his face, then press my hands firmly to his skin, forcing myself to meet the gaze of his two center-most eyes. All I can manage is a whisper, my voice cracking with agony. "I'm *not* her." I cough, then gasp at the pain as my flesh continues to burn. I force the words out. "But I-I'm s-sorry for w—"

He squeezes, cutting off my words. His eyes are wide, and he's trembling. In anger? I can't tell. The burns on my body scream with every tiny shift of my charred skin against his grip. I wish I would pass out. The pain is everywhere. We stay in this limbo for a few long seconds until he finally says, "What is this? What trick are you up to, Devana?"

I shake my head, but immediately stop, the agony nearly causing me to black out. "N-no one c-calls me that. I'm Ana. I'm not—"

A voice not my own cackles from my lips. The sound startles me, and I try to stop, but it keeps going. It's like my dream, but worse. I'm wide awake. I've been hijacked. My head tilts back all on its own, and I tsk at the monster. I try to tell him that I'm not in control, but what comes out of my mouth is, "Still so stupid. You could have killed me that night outside my cottage. You could have crushed my heart into dust and been done with me. But you didn't. You *couldn't*! And you could have killed me at any time these past few hours, but here we are. Tell me, do you still love me?"

I laugh maniacally, but tears of fear and frustration spill down my face. I really hate this bitch. How do I tell him this isn't me? He wouldn't believe me anyway. I wouldn't believe me if I were him. Still, I try to blink at the monster before me, urging him to see *me*. But black mist pours from my chest, peeling his grip off my body. I brace for the pain, knowing I can't stop myself from collapsing on the bed, but the mist surrounds me, and I land lightly on my feet.

My dress hangs in charred tatters, and I realize I no longer feel the horrifying red and black burns covering my skin. Maybe I'm going into shock?

Looking away from the nightmare that is my body, I scream at the monster. *Help! Help me! This isn't me!* But the words stay in my head. This, more than anything that has happened so far, is terrifying. I have no control. My body is no longer my own. It hurts. I'd rather face the monster and his wrath than let this Devana take over.

The deep, raspy female voice laughs in my head. *Do you think he would help you? That creature? I'm the reason he wants to kill you. And without me, without my magic, you would have died several times now. So be grateful. Sit back and give yourself to me.*

No!

Fight all you want, I'm stronger. I'll win in the end.

Without my permission, my feet move, and I take a few steps towards the monster. There is immense hate vibrating through me, but I know the feeling isn't mine.

I've never hated anything or anyone like this. And under the hate, there is ... hunger. Hunger for power. His power. She still wants it. She has wanted it for centuries, and she almost had it before he killed her and ripped out her heart.

I feel it in my chest. Her magic is gathering, spreading through me until it feels like there's not enough room for ... me.

This crazy bitch is going to try to kill him again. But she won't win. He's too strong. Unfortunately, it's my body that will die this time.

I don't want to die ...

... I'm just so tired.

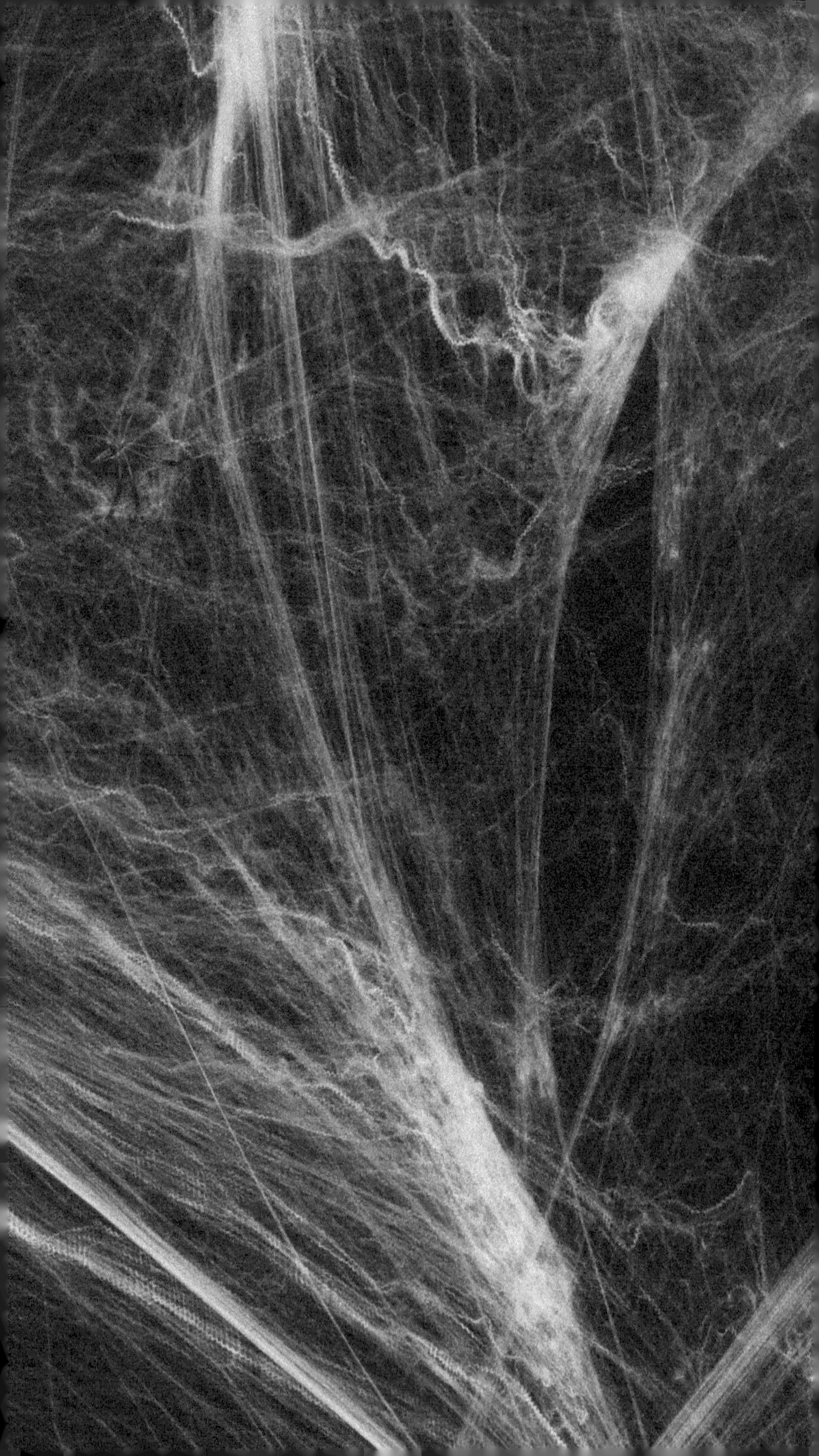

CHAPTER 12

THE ANCIENT

She has finally dropped the act and shown her true self.

Her voice has changed. Even the look in her eyes is different. I'm impressed with how perfectly she played the part of the innocent Ana for so long.

Ana. My mate.

It's confusing being bonded to this reincarnation, but I won't be deterred.

Even as I think that, the smell of her burnt flesh coats my nostrils and slicks down the back of my throat. It makes me sick. I did that to my mate.

No, I did that to *Devana.*

Her cackling laugh reaches a higher pitch, and the black mist around her explodes outward. Her magic slices into my skin, and I roar.

Good! Yes. Violence. I welcome her attack. This makes it easier.

With a burst of speed, I grab her, snarling in her face.

She smirks up at me, and I see red. I throw her. Hard. Everything seems to slow down as she crashes into the ruined balcony doors. Glass shatters and shards of wood go everywhere. I hide the wince that wants to pull at my face as several pieces of glass embed deeply into her flesh. A gash slices across her pale cheek, and her red-rimmed, shadowed eyes go wide with pain.

She lands with a sickening thud on the balcony, sliding several paces before coming to a limp stop. Blood flows from several wounds, one on her inner thigh practically gushing. The burns on her body reveal raw flesh, blackened at the edges.

Fuck, I hate this.

Her body jerks.

The black mist rises from her chest, molding around her body. Slowly, Devana's hair melts from sunset red to the raven black I recall. Her pretty dusting of freckles disappears from her nose as her skin darkens to a warm brown, and her hazel eyes change to gold as she glares at me.

Glass crunches under my feet as I stalk towards her. Pressing her hands to the stone, she attempts to push herself up, but her arms wobble then collapse. She's covered in blood. I should be delighted.

I'm not.

Her dark complexion wavers, slipping back to her Ana persona. Tears pool in her eyes that are still too golden as she reaches for me, her voice lighter and filled with pain. "Please. I don't want to die."

I glare down at her, unwilling to acknowledge the despair in my heart. "Don't bother with the fake tears. I'm not fooled, no matter how you change your appearance or what you call yourself." A single tear falls down her cheek as the wounds on her face begin to close, and I chuckle.

Of course, Devana would heal her face first, regardless of the fact that the cut on her leg is causing her to bleed out. "You're still so vain, Devana."

She rolls over, wincing as her burned flesh weeps blood and pus. Her tone once more goes deeper and turns rasping. "And you're still a fool." Her hair turns black once again, and all traces of *Ana* disappear. A grin lifts her lips, and she flexes her hand. I stagger back as my magic drains away. Glancing down, I rub at the glowing sigil on my chest. When did she put that there? I push my magic at the symbol to dispel it, but my power only siphons faster.

Devana laughs as the magic she's stealing from me lifts her off the floor. Her burns heal over, but blood still drips down her legs, the deepest of her wounds slower to close.

After all these years, I'm here again, in this goddess' clutches. Will I never learn? Of course, the Fates had to make things more difficult with this reincarnation by bonding us. Are they so bored that they're seeking entertainment through my suffering?

Well, fuck them, and fuck Devana. It may be hard to breathe as my magic pours from me with every beat of my heart, but I refuse to give in.

Devana's raven hair floats around her face, and her eyes glow with my power. She raises her arms, and the last of her ruined dress falls away. The moonlight streams over her blood-stained skin, now perfectly healed. She's beautifully horrendous. She's a monster ... and maybe that's why I loved her once upon a time.

Her arms drop, and for a moment, her eyes bleed to their pretty green, grey, and brown. Freckles dust her nose once more as she looks down at me from where she's floating on my magic. She has the gall to reach for me again. "Help."

Rage elongates my claws. "Fuck you, Devana. Stop. Just stop!"

A flicker of anger spills into her eyes. "I'm NOT—" Black hair and gold eyes take over once more, and her voice deepens. "Stay down, you bitch."

Wait. Is she ...

The roots of her hair turn red, and one eye goes green. She thrashes in the air, fighting ... nothing. Herself? What act is this?

She's distracted. Strike now.

Or is this a trap to draw me in?

She screams, "Leave me alone!" A loud smack sounds as she slaps herself. "Just give up!" "No! Get out!"

I gather my magic, ready to spear her through the heart, but as I do, my power drains. Ugh. The sigil. The more magic I use, the faster it's siphoned away.

Fine.

I settle my magic deep inside me where it's harder for Devana to get to. Just because I can't use my magic on her doesn't mean I can't kill her. Oh no. I'll rip her apart with my bare hands. Again.

She stops struggling, and she grins manically. Her hair is once again fully black, and her eyes are gold. Sudden panic nearly drives me to my knees. What if that was it? What if I don't see Ana again?

That's nonsense. It's an act. They are one and the same.

Her piercing gold gaze focuses on the empty space between us. "Oh! Oh, I see. How delicious. This little human thing is your mate." A snarl rumbles from my chest, but she just rolls her eyes. "This is perfect." Throwing back her head, her breasts shake with her laughter. "So that's why! You *literally* can't kill me. Your stupid monster biology is screaming at you to protect this body, isn't it?"

"It doesn't matter. I've rejected you. I've rejected the Fates. I think you'll find I can kill you just fine."

She tsks, pointing between us. "Come now, don't lie. I can see the thread tying you to this human. Disgusting." She flicks a lock of coal-black hair over her shoulder. "And for the record, *I'm* not your mate. She is, but she won't be around much longer. My soul is more powerful, and with your magic, she'll fade completely in a few moments."

Devana is lying. That's what she does.

Raising a hand, she wraps my magic around me, trying to immobilize me. Her finger taps the air in front of her, and a gold thread appears. It's beautiful, shimmering in the starlight, connecting our hearts.

Devana scrapes her nail along the string, and the bright light flickers, sending a pulse of pain through my chest. The hairs on the back of my neck stand up as she giggles darkly. "I think I'll cut it. I'd like to watch your face as I sever this ridiculous bond to her."

No.

She tilts her head. "You've rejected the bond, so maybe it won't hurt too badly. But I hope it does. I hope it's excruciating for you. Ooh! Maybe it will kill her! Let's find out."

She reaches for the dimming thread, and I feel my magic coalescing in her hand. She's going to do it. Devana is going to break the mate bond.

A roar erupts from me, shaking the balcony.

The goddess before me laughs.

Faster than a lightning strike, I'm before her. Grabbing her with my claws, I force my magic to yield to me, and me alone. This is *my* power, and Devana cannot have it. Just like she cannot have my mate. The glowing sigil waivers then shatters.

"Mine." My growl is deep and rumbling, and for one moment, hazel eyes stare up at me, tears in their depths. But then the color shifts back to gold, and Devana punches her magic at me. I snarl in pain, refusing to let go.

I fold space around us, moving us to the valley at the base of my mountain. My form expands until I tower over the highest peak. My voice booms like thunder. "You may be a goddess, Devana, but you are in my home, my realm, and you're trying to use *my* magic. You are outmatched. You shouldn't have come back."

She shoves her power against me once more, but this time it's a mere tickle along my palm.

I chuckle darkly. "You are done ruining my life or anyone else's, Devana."

With a growl, I shove my power down her throat. She gags, her gold eyes going wide. I feel them, the two souls warring in this body. Devana's dark mist swirls around the autumn-orange glow of the soul of my mate, trying to suffocate her, trying to blot her out of existence.

I didn't believe Ana when she told me she wasn't my Devana. How could I trust her? Still ... Oh, Fates. What have I done?

What I had to do. I'm not in the wrong here. Devana must die.

But maybe I can do it without sacrificing my mate?

Grabbing Devana's oily soul, I yank. Her body convulses, and dual gurgling screams rip from her throat. Boulders tumble down my mountain at her wails, but I keep pulling, praying this doesn't kill Ana. Lightning cracks, slamming into the ground, just barely missing me. Still, I continue to tear Devana out of my mate. Wind slashes at my skin, the earth trembles under my feet, and the forest actually weeps and groans. Devana *is* the goddess of nature and the forest. She is also the goddess of ...

I look up, noticing a red haze over the moon.

With a bellow, I pour more of my magic into her, yanking until I hear harsh tearing sounds. Her bloody screams seem to carry across the entire realm. As I pull Devana out, Ana's body goes limp in my grip, her hair turning fully red, her hazel eyes closing, her head lolling back.

The goddess's soul writhes in my other hand, the black gossamer tendrils biting into my flesh like vipers. Using my two free arms, I sink my claws into Devana and shred. I tear, and rend, and destroy until there's nothing left but miniscule, whimpering pieces of smoke.

I'm not satisfied. It's not enough.

Gathering the sad remainders of Devana's soul into my palms, I set them on fire, watching as they burn with tiny screams of pain. As the last piece sizzles and burns away, I sigh, dropping my arms.

I don't know if she's completely gone—she is a goddess—but at the very least, she's gone for a long, long while ... Hopefully, forever.

Shrinking my form, I step through another portal, cradling my blood-covered mate in my arms. Her face is too pale. The only thing keeping my panic at bay is the faint gold glow of the thread between us.

Taking extra care, I try to ease the tension in my body, concentrating on keeping my claws from cutting into her. My body tingles. I'm restless and on the verge of burning everything down to keep this little human alive and safe. Mine. Mine. Mine.

But will she ever really be yours? You failed to believe

*her and hurt her so many times, physically and emotion-
ally. You're a monster.*

I snarl at my thoughts as I watch her chest barely lift
with her weak breaths. Her heart flutters, kicks into a
desperate gallop, then ... stops.

No.

The world around me disappears. My body shakes
with absolute terror.

I must be careful. If I push too much of my magic into
her, she may disintegrate right here in my arms. Slowly, I
feed my magic to her, like little sips of water. I manage to
take in a breath as her heart restarts with a faint thud.

Holding her against my chest, I cross the balcony and
step into my bedchamber. Broken glass tinkles underfoot,
and the flames in the fireplace still burn silently, bright,
and warm.

I stare at her face in awe ... and trepidation.

I rejected her. My mate nearly died. There are dark
smudges under her eyes, and her lips are chapped.
Devana may have healed her body, but I don't know how
to heal the emotional damage I've dealt her.

Maybe I can erase or replace her memories of me, but
that voice in my head says, *You can't keep betraying your
mate. Be the male she needs you to be.*

Tilting my head back, I growl at the ceiling. "Fates!
Why did it have to be Devana? Why couldn't you just
send me my mate without the spirit of a psychotic goddess
attached like a leech?"

*Trying to pass the blame? You rejected her the moment
you knew she was your mate ... before you knew she was
Devana. This is all your fault.*

With that admonishment swirling through my head, I
lower Ana towards the bed, but stop. With a pulse of my
magic, I clean the blood from her skin, clear the dust from

the room, and fluff the comforter and pillows. My powers wipe away the cobwebs, repair the glass in the balcony doors, freshen the white paint on the two plaster walls, remove the moisture from the exposed rock of the other walls and ceiling, then tie back the heavy midnight curtains. Using one of my hands, I pull back the blankets and settle my mate in my bed.

Our bed.

I trace a claw down her tear-stained cheek. Brushing her messy curls away from her face, I pull a soft blanket over her, covering her naked body. I clench and unclench my hands, hovering, not sure what to do.

My mate.

Devana wasn't my mate ... not even close ... but I can't help wondering if Ana will break my heart too.

Never again? No, I think I'd let her. She might be worth it.

I should leave and let her rest, give her space. I should at least sit on the other side of the room to keep watch over her in case she wakes and needs ... anything.

Closing my eyes, I magic away my horns to make it more comfortable to lie on my side. Carefully, I climb into the bed, curling around Ana, holding her with all four of my arms, my tail curling around her thigh.

She still smells faintly of blood, sweat, dirt ... and my saliva. I just barely hold back a pained groan as I recall her rolling around in my mouth as I tried to fucking eat her. Fuck.

My racing heart slows when I catch the scent of apples and honey—a scent all her own. My mate. I pull her against me, syncing my breaths with hers, eager for her to wake, but dreading that moment she does open her eyes.

CHAPTER 13

ANA

I'm tired. So tired. I'm warm and there's a sense of safety, but my insides feel like I was ripped apart and put back together. I think maybe I was.

I sink deeper into the darkness, away from the pain. I ignore the little voice in my head telling me to get up, to run, to fight, to do ... something. I'm just too tired. Even my soul feels drained. My limbs are heavy, and no amount of willpower will open my eyes. Did Devana win? Is this what it feels like to be overtaken? To disappear?

I don't hear her anymore. In fact, I don't feel her at all.

A deep voice—his voice—whispers, *Little sprite, open your eyes.*

A tingling warmth surrounds me, and that sense of safety deepens, but I wonder if this feeling of security is false. I'm tired of fighting. I want to go home, but the darkness, the nothingness is soothing. It's easier to stay here.

I sink deeper.

I'm exhausted.

I drift away, feeling like I'm floating on my back in the waters of a becalmed sea at night with no stars or moon to light the way.

I float until my thoughts fade, until *I* fade.

On and on, there's nothing.

"Little sprite, you must wake."

That voice. It tugs at my soul, and I want to follow it. But I'm also afraid. If I go, will I just be returning to more terror? No. No more running. No more fear. No more. I turn away from the voice and cling to the darkness.

I can't breathe. I sputter and choke, curling in on myself.

"It has been three turns, little sprite. If you won't wake, you must at least drink."

I swallow, and as the voice fades, so do I, back into the void.

Water cools my throat once more. How long have I been in the darkness?

I fade. Who am I?

Red. Twin pinpoints of glowing red eyes pierce the endless dark. They hover in the distance for a long moment before they start moving closer. More eyes blink open as the monster approaches. I thought I was safe here in my mind, but of course he found me.

"I have left you alone for too long, thinking you needed time. Enough, little sprite. Wake up. Now."

I sigh. "This is all in my head. You're not real. I'm tired. Leave me alone."

I blink, and he's before me. In the darkness, I can barely make out the faint outline of his body, his horns, his four arms, and the shadowy swish of his tail. His eyes, though, his eyes are brilliant, like little pools of molten lava.

"Yes, we are in your mind, but this is real. I am here, and you must wake. You are too weak. You are fading."

I shrug, turning away.

His voice drops to a whisper. "Little sprite, I'm ... I ..."

Something in me aches at the despair in his words. I don't want to feel sorry for him. I don't want to feel anything. Pulling at the darkness, I wrap it around myself.

A roar shakes the shadows as claws grip my shoulders. "WAKE UP!"

With a painful gasp, I lurch upright, clutching my chest. I can't catch my breath, and my hands are shaking. Fabric slides around my shoulders, and when I glance down, a thin blanket settles over my naked body. The burns are gone. In fact, not a single scratch marks my skin. I recall crashing through the balcony doors and the agony as several glass shards lodged in my body. There was so much pain. But it's all gone now.

Gone but not forgotten.

When I lift my head, dozens of blazing eyes stare down at me from where the monster sits perched on the edge of the giant bed I'm in. Three of his hands clench in the bedding as one hand reaches for me. I don't flinch. I don't move, staying still like the prey I am. He stops a few inches from touching my face, then drops his hand.

"Good, you are awake."

He turns, picking up a bowl. I inhale the scents of salt, carrots, onion, and garlic, and my mouth waters. The spoon handle looks tiny in his giant hand as he scoops up the clear broth. The monster, the giant horned monster who hunted me and tried to kill me, actually blows on the soup a few times before holding it out to me.

I blink. My gaze snaps between the spoon and his face, then I blurt out, "You were in my head."

He nods, sending his silver hair swishing against his bare chest. "It was necessary. You would not wake."

I drop my gaze, and my fingers worry at the blanket. Through my lashes, I watch as he puts the spoon back in the bowl, and his many eyes stare at the top of my head. For a moment, it looks like he's going to say something, but then he sighs.

I lift my gaze as he grabs the spoon once more, scooping up some broth and blowing on it again. When he holds it before my lips, my stomach growls, but I resist leaning forward to take the spoon into my mouth. Instead, I press back against the headboard. "No. This is a trick."

He doesn't move except for the slight tilt of his head. "Trick?"

Worried that the bitch, Devana will take over again at any moment, I rush my words. "You can't kill me with *her* magic protecting me, so you're trying to poison me."

He frowns, scooting closer. A few drops of broth land on the blanket, and I seal my lips shut as he brings the spoon closer to my mouth.

Shaking my head, I tick off reasons on my fingers why I don't trust him. "You hunted me for hours on end, you tried to fucking eat me, you chased me some more, you tried to crush me, burn me, and you threw me off a balcony then through a glass door. I hate Divana, but if killing her means I have to die too ... I'm not eating that."

He frowns, using one of his hands to rake his claws through his silver hair. "This is no trick, little sprite. The goddess is gone. She is no longer inside you. You are ... I'm simply trying to feed you. You need to rebuild your strength."

Goddess? She was an actual goddess? There was a goddess inside me? And this monster, what? Killed her? Exorcized her? How do you kill a goddess?

Thankfully, all that stays inside my head, and in response to my silence, he says, "You have been asleep for seven turns." My brows furrow, and he says, "Seven days."

Seven days! No wonder I'm so weak. A horrified thought makes me shift to the side, and I glance down at the bed. It's clean.

He says, "My magic cleaned away your—"

I hold up a hand, stalling his words. I don't need to hear how he cleaned up my bodily functions while I was unconscious. *He was taking care of me?* We stare at each other for a long moment. He's being ... kind, but I recall every terrifying moment since I landed in this place, and my heartbeat quickens.

He leans forward. Bracing one of his hands on the headboard, another wraps around my hip over the sheet. I'm too dizzy to dodge his third hand, and he grips my chin.

And now my heart is racing for a completely different reason, and my pussy clenches. *Jesus, Ana, get a grip.*

But then he squeezes my face and forces my mouth open. "You must eat."

I try to shake my head, but his grip is too strong. I don't trust him. For some reason I want to, but I can't afford to. The spoon clinks against my teeth, and the delicious broth floods my mouth. My tongue rolls with the urge to swallow, but I don't.

He slides the spoon from between my lips, then dips his head so our noses nearly touch. "Swallow."

I give him my best glare, ignoring the heat pooling between my thighs at the intensity in his gaze and the way he growled that single word.

Inappropriate, Ana.

The broth sitting in my mouth is so good. I really want to drink down the entire bowl, but ...

I spit the soup out, spraying the liquid all over his face and chest.

He doesn't even flinch, which is annoying. The next second he's suddenly clean, all signs of my little outburst gone from his skin. A sigh huffs from his lips, and then he shoves my head back until I'm staring at the ceiling. Tears pool in my eyes. My neck aches, and my jaw will probably have bruises. He pours more broth into my mouth then pinches my nose, repeating his command. "Swallow, Ana."

And I do, my body melting as the warm soup slides down my throat. He just said my name. Not Devana said in anger or revulsion. He called me Ana.

And I liked it.

A lot.

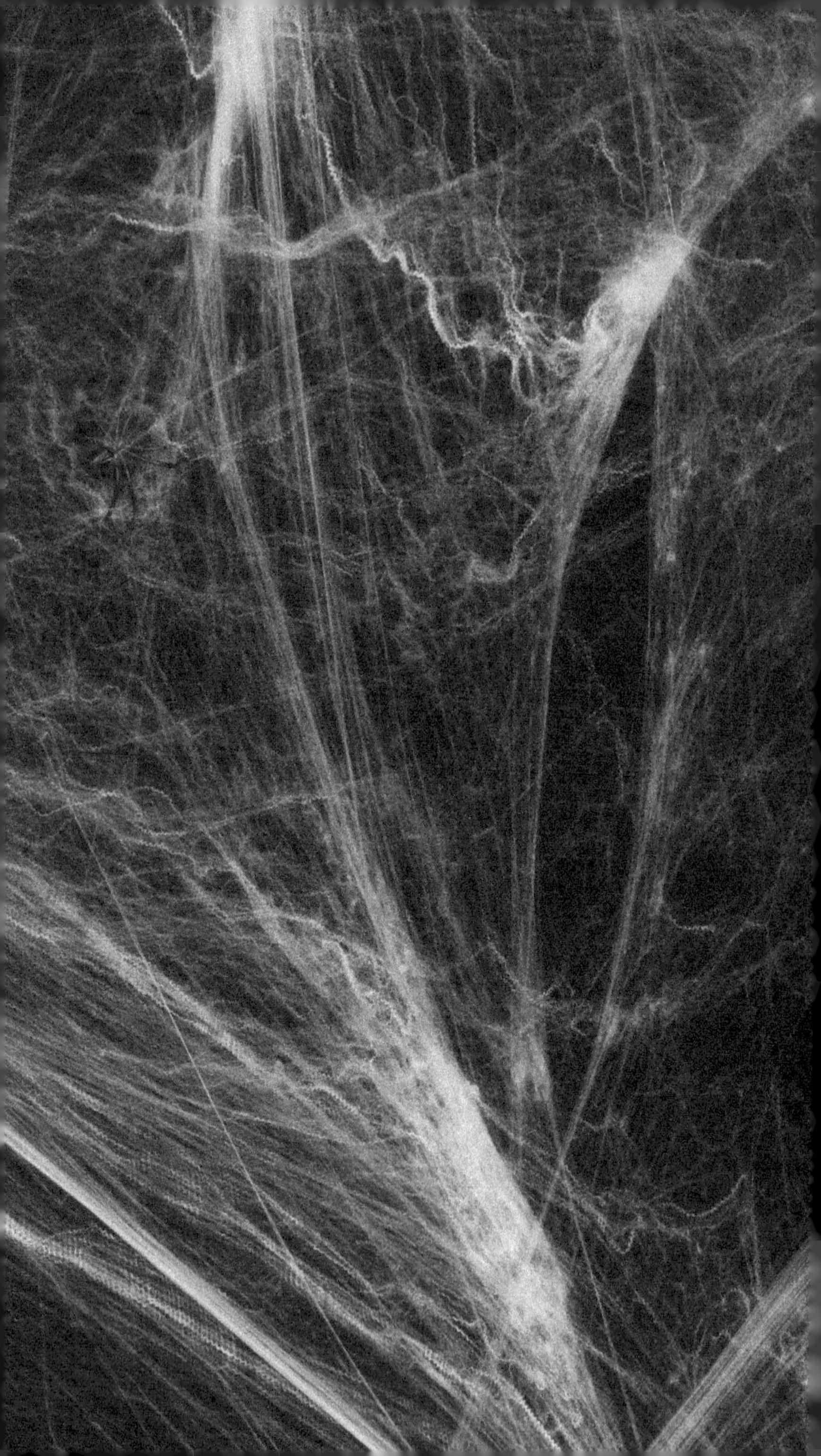

CHAPTER 14

THE ANCIENT

I hate forcing her ... but I like it.

My gaze locks on her throat as she swallows, and I can't help but think of what else I want her to swallow. Once I release her face, she coughs, slumping forward. Instinctually, I rub her back over the sheet.

While Devana was inhabiting her, the goddess' magic kept my mate in this realm. And after, my magic has been holding her here, preventing The Divide from pulling her back to the human realm. That's what it does. The Divide sets everything right, making sure monsters are in the monster realm, and humans are in the human realm.

But once I claim her, I won't need to use my magic. She will be bound to me, and not even The Divide can separate us.

Ana trembles with each cough. She's too thin. I will force her back to full health and then I will claim her.

This little human will love me. She will warm my bed and give me her body.

Her coughs subside, but her head remains bowed, and I realize I'm still rubbing her back. Touching her is ... calming.

You know you have no right to lay your hands on her.

She's mine, my mate.

But after what you put her through ...

I ignore my inner conflict as I say, "More. You must eat more for your health."

She shakes her head. "No."

Before I realize what I'm doing, my hands wrap around her shoulders, and I give her a little shake, and her teeth clatter.

Gently. Gently. This is not how you will win her over ... no matter how difficult she's being.

I force myself to soften my grip, my thumbs rubbing back and forth on her skin where the sheet slid down a few inches. "Please."

"No."

"Fine!" I push off the bed, needing to put distance between us before I hold her down and pour the entire bowl of soup down her throat.

I reach for the door handle, but her voice stops me. "Okay." There's a long pause, and when I don't move, she continues, "Okay. I ... I guess it didn't kill me, so ..."

Still facing away from her, I smile with my little victory before I turn, wiping the grin away so she doesn't see. The sheets shift as she bends her legs, hugging her knees to her chest. This time, when I hold out the spoon, she opens her mouth. I salivate at the sight of my mate before me, in my bed, lips parted.

I tried to reject this?

The golden thread pulled between us shimmers. It's not as bright as before, but it's still there, and it comforts me. She's still mine.

Ana takes two more spoonfuls before she asks, "Why do you call me, little sprite?"

A soft smile lifts my lips. "Because when I first saw you, you had wings."

She groans. "My costume."

"I assume it was an All Hallows Eve thing?"

She nods. "How did I get here?"

"Magic."

She snorts a laugh. It's a nice sound—silly and happy. "Well, I got that, but like, how?"

"Obviously, something in your world pushed you here, or Devana's magic pulled you across The Divide."

"Why me?"

I shrug. "You share a name, maybe you share a lineage."

"Ugh. I've always hated my name. That's why I go by Ana. *Devana.* So dramatic. I was named after the Slavic goddess of the hunt and the moon." She pauses, her eyes going wide as if she's just now putting the pieces together. "Wait, you said that thing inside me was a goddess. Was that ..?"

I nod. "Yes, or at the very least, she was an aspect of Devana. Originally, she was just a simple witch with average power. But people started claiming her magic was Divine. Devana quickly gathered worshipers, and she turned their devotion and prayers into power. Eventually, Devana's magic got so strong, she became the goddess her people claimed her to be. She was always power hungry, and when the old Slavic gods started to fall out of favor, her magic waned. So, she went searching for more. She found it in the many realms available to magic wielders."

"And then she found you."

"And then she found me."

Her eyes hold sadness as she focuses behind me. "Why is it always night?"

I'm grateful for her abrupt change of topic, all too willing to talk about something else. The spoon clinks against the bowl as I scoop up more broth. "Eat."

She obeys, but keeps her gaze averted. I nod as she swallows the broth. "We don't have a sun here in Ekenys."

"Ekenys?"

"What you call, the monster realm." My gaze travels over her body and the thin sheet wrapped around her. "It is much colder here. Do you require more warmth?"

She shrugs, but I notice the little bumps raised along her exposed skin, so I make the silent flames in the fireplace larger and create a thicker blanket with my magic. She doesn't lift her head from where it's perched on her knees as I drape it over her shoulders.

Why won't she look at me? I am caring for her. I'm feeding her and looking after her. She was talking and asking questions. Why has she closed herself off?

"Little sprite?" I abhor the desperation in my voice.

She hugs herself tighter. "I want to go home."

My heart plummets into my stomach. My Ana ... leave? No. She's my mate. She will come to understand she belongs here with me. I need her to stay, so I tell a small lie. "You are still too weak to cross The Divide. Humans are frail enough, but in your current state, crossing would be very painful, maybe even deadly."

Sure, it might be a little uncomfortable for her to cross, but I'm more than powerful enough to easily take her back to her realm. Or I could simply let go of my magic and let The Divide rip her away from me. I don't tell her that, though.

I expect outrage or for her to hit me with a barrage of questions. Instead, she flops onto her side, curling into a tight ball.

I reach for her, giving her shoulder a soft squeeze. "You must eat more."

With a huff, she pushes onto her elbow and snatches the bowl from me. The broth spills down her chin as she tips it back and drinks the rest down. She tosses the bowl to the end of the bed, then collapses back onto her side. "There. Happy? I'm tired. Please leave."

"Little sprite, I don't think—"

Pulling the blanket over her head, she mumbles, "Whatever. Do what you want. Just let me sleep."

My heart aches to give my mate what she wants, but I can't have her slipping back into the void. I might not be able to reach her next time. She was so weak, floating away in the darkness of her mind. There was so much despair. She was on the verge of giving up. I was almost too late.

I easily lift her from the bed, blanket and all. She squeaks, kicking her feet, but her arms automatically wrap around my neck. *Yes. This is good. This is right.* I use one of my hands to push the blanket off her head, and it pools around her shoulders. Her cheeks turn pink with a blush, causing her freckles to stand out as she asks, "What are you doing?"

"Taking care of you." And it feels right. I know it's the mate bond driving me to see to her needs, but after these past several days of looking after her, I find I'm happy to do it.

"Taking care of me? After you tried to kill me ... several times?"

I pause in the doorway, words of apology lodged in my throat.

I have nothing to be sorry for.

Yes, you do, and you know it.

And if I do say the words, what if she rejects me?

She should after what you did to her.

I keep silent, and with a flick of my magic, I open a portal and step through to the thermal caves deep within my mountain. As I stride into the nearest steaming pool, I magic away her blanket. The moment our skin touches, my body reacts. The frills along my cock flutter and vibrate. I walk us into the hot water and get harder at the moan of pleasure she releases. "Oh god, that feels so good."

My mate melts against me, and I can't stop a purr from rumbling my chest.

I lower myself onto a ledge, cradling Ana in two of my arms as the others stroke her hair. Carefully, my fingers work through the knots and tangles. I have to take special care with the snarled braids, undoing them one at a time. She's silent as I massage her scalp, letting her fiery hair spill through my fingers. Her eyes are closed, and her mouth is slightly parted. All I want is to adjust her until she's positioned over my aching cock and let her slide down my length.

Instead, I turn her and place her on the ledge. She opens her hazel eyes, not bothering to cover herself. I fist my hands to keep from cupping her small breasts and teasing her nipples. Now is not the time.

I back away, distracting myself by focusing on the water rippling around my tense body. I guess I'm going to try this apology thing, but I can't say what I need to with the temptation of her soft skin touching mine.

"Little sprite, I ..."

The words stick like thorns in my throat. I'm an

Ancient. I don't say, I'm sorry. I don't apologize. I am powerful. I am respected. I am feared.

And that's the problem. I made my mate fear me.

Her whisper seems to caress the mist curling around us. "You ... you loved her. You obviously hated her deeply, but it was because of your love and how she betrayed you."

"How ...?"

Her fingers dig into her wet hair, scraping along her scalp. "I saw it. Her memories ... of you." She taps her temple. "In here."

She saw, but she doesn't *understand*. How could she? I haven't explained anything.

My powerful legs carry me through the water until I'm back before her. I kneel, the water lapping around my chest, and as I do, I shift into a human form. I hate it, but this body should make my sprite more comfortable, so I'll endure it.

"Little sprite, I—"

"Don't."

My gaze snaps her face. Her lips tremble, but then she bites them. I reach out, realizing I'm shaking as I brush the back of my knuckles over her cheek. "Don't what, little sprite?"

"Don't pretend to be human. Not that. Just ... What do you really look like? Show me?"

I'm blown away by her words. She wants the monster? She wants me?

Ana bravely holds my gaze, her eyes conveying an expectation as if she believes me to be the kind of male who will kneel before her and apologize. I am already kneeling ...

I'm sorry. Say it. Say it, you fool.

I sigh, scratching the back of my neck. "To be honest,

I don't recall what my original form looks like. I've lived a long time, and I've taken many forms."

"Then give me what feels the most like you. It seems only fair. I'm here. I want to run. I should run, but something … I'm just … Don't be human. Please?"

Hope stirs in my heart. She feels it. Our bond. She doesn't understand, but she will.

My human form melts away, and I'm once again the dark monster of her nightmares. All I can do is watch with my lips parted as she leans forward. Her fingers pinch the long strands of my silver hair before letting them fall back into the water. "That's better."

"You really prefer … this?"

"It's who you are, yes?" I nod, and she nods in return. "Then, yes."

Amazing. This little human woman is amazing.

Still on my knees, I crawl forward until my stomach presses to her shins. I was wrong before. I need to touch her as I say this. Two of my hands land on her thighs. She tenses slightly, but I'm relieved when she doesn't shift away from my touch.

"Little sprite, I … I am … I am so …"

Holding my gaze, she says nothing. She waits. As I look into my mate's green, brown, and grey eyes, the pressure in my chest melts away. I will give her anything. I will do anything for her, even say I'm sorry.

"Little sprite." I shake my head. "No. *Ana*, I am sorry." A frown pulls at my lips. As hard as those words were to say, now that I've said them, they don't feel adequate. "But words are not enough, so perhaps over time, my actions will speak for me, and I can *show* you how sorry I am."

Her hands slide over mine where they still rest on her bare thighs. The heat of the water creates little beads of sweat that sparkle on her skin like tiny jewels. The steam curls and dances around us, hiding her face from me for a moment. Once the cloud of mist clears, I find myself once again staring into her hazel eyes.

She licks her lips, and my cock twitches as she says, "Show me, how?"

CHAPTER 15

ANA

Heat pools in my cheeks. I know I'm blushing. Did I just ask him how he'd show me how sorry he was? Out loud?

He chuckles, and the sound sends tingles deep inside me. "Oh, little sprite, the things that come to mind ..."

I'm so wet, and not just from the deliciously hot water lapping at my neck and shoulders. He licks his lips, and I notice his tongue is more pointed than a human's. And long. Very long.

Terror slices down my spine as I recall his jaws closing in around me. The fear of that memory shifts and feeds my desire. Fear and lust. The combination is quite the aphrodisiac, and I'm aching. His fingers tighten on my thighs, and I realize this is the smallest his form has ever been. I mean, he's still huge, but his hands don't wrap all the way around my legs like they would have earlier.

He shakes his head. "But ..."

"*But? No but.*" There I go, thinking out loud again.

He laughs, and his smile makes the red glow of his eyes sparkle. "*But*, first, you need to rest. You also need to eat and regain your strength."

Oh yeah. Now that he's drawn attention back to it, the trembling in my body intensifies. My arms are both too heavy and too light. My stomach feels hollow. And on top of all that, I'm ... desperately needy.

I shift away from his touch, trying to remind myself this isn't one of my fantasy books. I hug my knees to my chest, bracing my feet on the ledge. Trying to hide my body as much as I can, I whisper, "It doesn't make sense."

"What doesn't, little sprite?"

"The way I feel. About you. It's confusing. You wanted to kill me. It was terrifying." He frowns, but I continue. "And now ... You're taking care of me. You're being ... sweet. And I like it. Why am I not more afraid right now? My brain can't keep up. It's making me dizzy. Or, I guess that could be the lack of food over the past seven days."

"You are dizzy?" He reaches for me with real concern in his many eyes.

I wave him off. "I'm fine. Well, not fine, but ..." I tilt my head, hugging myself a little tighter. "Why are you doing this? Why are you even keeping me around? With your Devana, the body stealing goddess gone, I'd think you'd be itching to get rid of the pesky human who was dropped in your lap."

He growls, his hand snatching my chin, holding me prisoner to his gaze as he says, "First, she wasn't *my* anything. Not for over a century. And even then, I think ... no, I *know* I romanticized what I felt for her. It made it easier to hate her. And I did. I do. But, Ana, I didn't love her. I know that now."

"You didn't?"

His silver hair swirls in the water, and I sink into his hold, too eager for his answer.

"No." *Because what I felt for her doesn't hold a candle to what I feel for you.*

I imagine those words floating on the mist. I see them in his eyes. But that's absurd.

He leans even closer. His breath fans over my cheeks as he says, "And second, you dropping into my lap is the best thing that's ever happened to me in all my thousands of years of existence."

Oh my. I mentally fan myself as I say, "Thousands?" He nods, his lips so close to mine, I keep darting glances to his dark mouth. "That can't ... I'm not anyone spec—"

Another of his hands slides along my shoulder until his fingers circle my neck. He doesn't squeeze or grip, he just holds me. "You are human, so you can't understand, but you are mine."

I'm not an object. I don't belong to anyone. That thought is not as emphatic as it should be, because the desire in his eyes stirs the lust and lingering fear inside me until I'm throbbing between my thighs.

His voice drops even deeper. "When I first saw you, I had every intention of denying you, of rejecting us." His claws scrape the edges of my throat, and for some reason it makes me want to tilt my head back to give him better access. "And learning that Devana's soul was inside you made it easy to reject you. At least, that's what I told myself."

With a little tug, he pulls me forward and my legs fall back to the ledge. He whispers in my ear. "But there's no resisting you, Ana. I am yours. Your mate. We are fated."

Woah, what? My hands land on his chest. I push, and he obliges, shifting back enough so I can see his face as I say, "Fated? Like, fated mates? Like in stories? That can't be real. Mates? No. No. Surely not. You—"

This is too much. Fated?

He closes the distance between us once more, only this time he doesn't pull me to him, he bends to me. His lips press to mine, and that purring sound rumbles from his chest. As he adjusts his mouth to suck on my bottom lip, his purr changes to a rumbling growl. I gasp at the flood of carnal hunger that punches through me. He takes the opening and plunges his tongue into my mouth. His hands are everywhere, but the one stays around my throat, directing me where he wants me.

This monster tried to kill you.

He said he was sorry.

You're really just going to ignore all the red flags because he said sorry?

And he's a fucking good kisser.

I internally roll my eyes at myself, then all thoughts shut down as one of his hands holds the back of my head, taking the kiss deeper. Another hand curls under my ass, squeezing.

The image of his impressive cock spears through my mind. What do those frills feel like? My hand starts to trail down his chest, but he pulls away from the kiss. He pants as he shakes his head, two of his hands falling away, the other two coming back to my thighs. I peek through the water, and ... holy shit! Is the water making him look bigger? It must be. My hips involuntarily roll as those goddamn frills flare and flutter along his hard length.

He clears his throat, and I snap my gaze to his face, caught red-handed. I can't keep the blush from my face, but luckily, he doesn't call me out. Instead, he says, "I shouldn't have done that. You need your rest. You are still weak."

No! Don't stop. I manage to keep that plea to myself as I fight to calm down. Funny, I don't feel weak at all right now. I'm just really, really turned on.

He rubs two of his hands together, and I assume magically, suds foam between his fingers. He brings his hands to my scalp and starts massaging as he says, "Let me finish what I brought you here for. Then, will you try to eat a bit more for me?"

My stomach grumbles, and I press a palm to my middle. "I know that soup wasn't much, but I feel full and hungry at the same time. And kinda nauseated."

"Hmm. Maybe we will wait to try solid food until after you drink some water and have rested a bit."

I didn't feel tired a moment ago, but his fingers working through my hair now have me melting, and suddenly, a nice long nap doesn't sound so bad.

My eyes close as he rinses my hair, then starts smearing something sweet-smelling from my roots to the tips. I startle, my eyes opening as the water starts to fizz and bubble around us like champagne. The tingles make me feel clean and refreshed. Once again, he rinses my hair, then he scoops me into his arms. As he carries me out of the pool, I hold up a hand, noticing my fingers are wrinkled but my skin is dry and clean.

I blink, and I'm back in his bed. *"Did I fall asleep, or did he portal us here?"*

"You fell asleep, little sprite."

"Oh, I said that out loud, didn't I?"

He chuckles, tucking me in. Who is this monster who displays such tenderness?

His fingers linger as he stands. He's going to leave, which is probably for the best. I need to get out of here. I need to go home. But ...

I reach out, curling my fingers as far as they will go

around his wrist. He looks at where I've gripped him, and I blurt out, "Stay." His jaw flexes as he looks between my face and my hand on his arm. I see his hesitance, so I pull out the big guns, pushing out my bottom lip just a little. "Please."

His shoulders slump ... in relief? In resignation? "Okay, little sprite."

When he reaches for the chair, I tug on his arm. He looks back at me, and I pat the bed. This is crazy. What am I doing? Why do I feel like I'd sleep better with him beside me? Is this stockholm syndrome? I vaguely recall reading somewhere that isn't an actual thing ... but here I am.

He shakes his head, and hot tears burn my throat as he says, "I don't think that's a good idea. You are safe, and I won't be far. Rest well." Is he rejecting me after all? And why does that thought hurt like I'm being torn in two? This can't be real, can it?

A portal opens, and I'm about to call out to him, only to realize I don't know his name.

Red flags as far as the eye can see.

As he disappears, a soft shirt forms around my body. It hangs to mid-thigh and smells like him ... like wood smoke and snow. I've never seen him in any kind of clothing, making me believe the scent on this shirt is intentional. He left, but he left a little piece of himself here with me.

Still, he left, and that ... hurts. He's a big, scary, terrifying monster—a monster who looked after me, fed me, bathed me, washed my hair, and tucked me into bed. He said he was sorry.

He's still a monster.

He makes me feel things.

I pull the neck of the shirt over my nose and bury my

face in the fabric, curling into a pillow. A few words of apology and one killer kiss should not be enough to have me ready to forgive and forget. Well, I doubt I'll forget, but my pussy really wants me to forgive.

Fated mates.

That's what he said. We are fated. But that's just something that only happens in stories, right?

You mean stories where monsters invade your world every day? Stories where you are magically whisked away to another realm right into the arms of the one fated to be yours? Stories like the ones you read one handed as you get yourself off?

I blush at my thoughts.

My voice is muffled in the shirt as I say to myself, "I guess it's not totally out of the question ... but regardless if it's true or not, he obviously thinks it *is*. Does that mean he intends to keep me here? Even against my will?"

Do you want to go home?

"Yes."

But?

"But I also want to know ..."

What if it is true?

A wistful sigh leaves me. "What if it's true?"

I take another inhale of his scent, snuggling deeper. First thing first. I need to ask him his name ...

A yawn cracks my jaw.

... when I wake up.

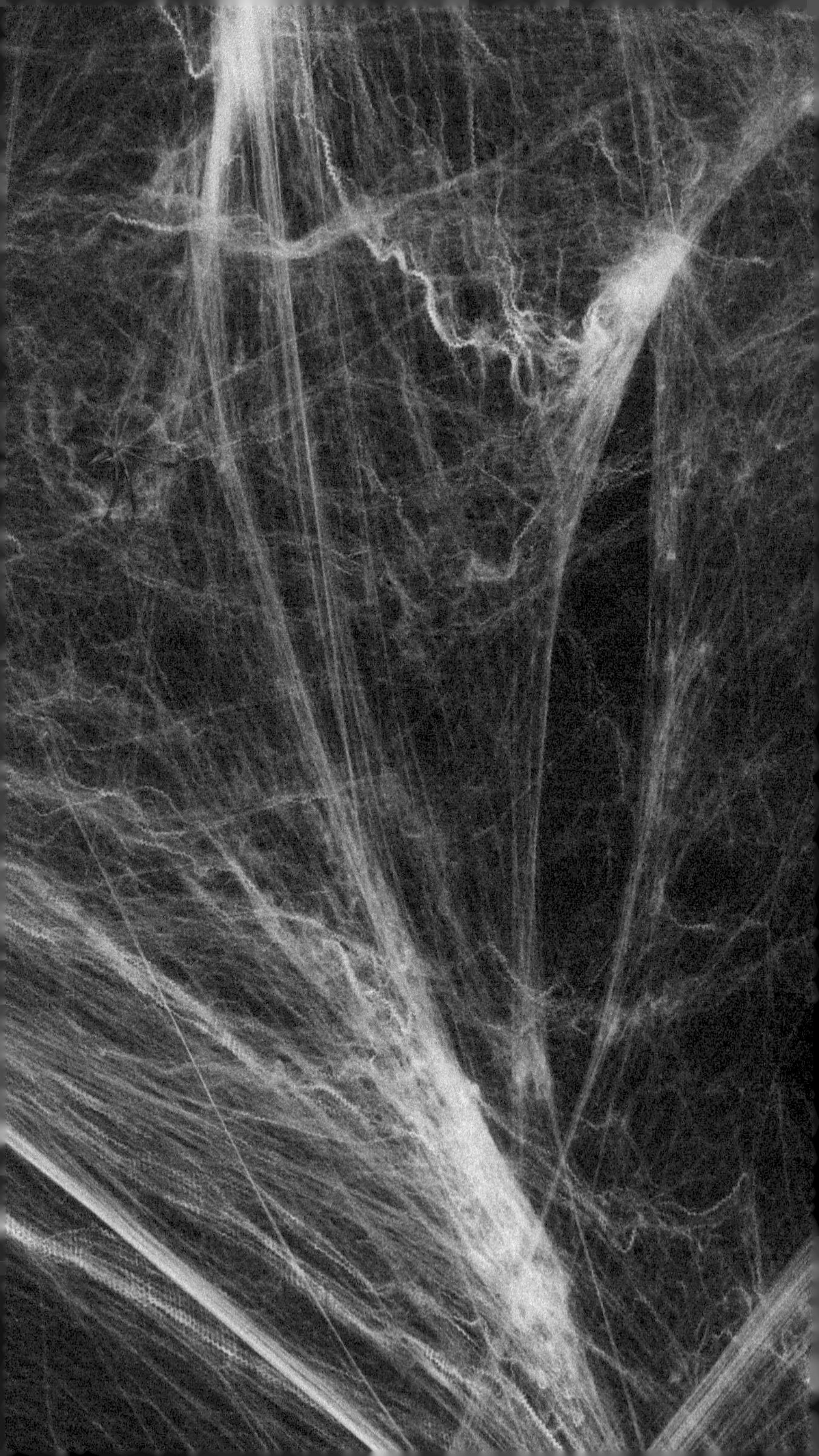

CHAPTER 16

THE ANCIENT

The meditation music goes silent, and I jump to my feet as Ana's scream tears through my mountain. I rip open a portal, leaping into my bedchamber, ready to kill ... anything, everything.

Ana thrashes in the bed, the blankets kicked aside, the large shirt I gave her bunched around her waist. A quick scan of the room reveals we are alone. My gaze travels down her exposed lower half. Oh, to be able to slide my tail up those legs to tease at her entrance, to prod, to stroke. How wet would she get for me?

"No. Please, no." Her soft whimpers snap my attention to her face. She's dreaming. She's having a nightmare. About me?

Of course about me.

I take a step towards her, but pause. What do I do? I want to comfort her. I need to. But I am her nightmare, so how ...?

"Please, help me. Get her out. I'm not her. Please see I'm not her."

Wait, she's dreaming about Devana? The relief I feel goes bone deep. But then, Ana screams again. Her little hands come to her throat, and nail marks score down her neck.

I'm at her side before I realize I've moved. "Little sprite, wake up. You're having a nightmare. You're safe." I stroke her hair, and for a second she relaxes, but then her back arches, and her body goes stiff. Scooping her into my arms, I press my lips to her ear. "You are not her. I see you, Ana. You are safe. Wake up."

She's so warm. She feels good in my arms. I berate myself for ever thinking this woman was Devana. My hate blinded me. I knew it and ignored it. I tried to use my grudge as a shield to protect my heart.

As she slowly relaxes, I nuzzle her neck. "I'm such a fool. My heart was never mine to protect. It is yours."

She moans. There's pain in the soft sound, and it makes my heart ache. But then she turns into me, rubbing her cheek against my chest. I hold still as she presses a palm to my torso. Her hand trembles slightly, reminding me how weak and fragile she is. I don't dare move. I barely breathe out of fear she will pull away, or worse, scream and run. In this state, I doubt she can even stand, but the thought of chasing her makes my mouth water.

"How long was I out this time?" Her voice is low and scratchy, and it makes my tail flick.

"Just a few hours. You were having a nightmare, otherwise I would have let you sleep longer."

"A nightmare?"

I nod. "Do you feel any better?"

"Mhm." Her eyes blink open, and she looks up at my

face. "What's your name? I keep calling you, monster, in my head, but that seems ... rude."

I chuckle, running my fingers through her hair. "It is true though. I am a monster. And I was particularly monstrous towards you."

"Yeah, well." She shifts to sit up, then pauses to catch her breath. After a moment, she crosses her legs, tucking her shirt around her thighs. I lick my lips, captured by the movement of her fingers along the hem of the material skimming her bare legs. She clears her throat, and when I look at her face, a pretty pink stains her cheeks. She covers her mouth with a hand as she says, "My breath is atrocious. I don't suppose you have a spare toothbrush, or maybe there's a monster convenience store nearby?"

I cock my head to the side. Her breath smells fine to me, but if my mate is uncomfortable ... I wave a hand, magically cleaning her mouth. Her eyes go wide, and she runs her tongue along her teeth.

That nearly undoes me. I'm a second away from pushing her back onto my bed and fucking her senseless, but she smiles and says, "Mint. That's really cool. Thanks."

"You're welcome."

Mimicking her, I scoot back to make room so I can cross my legs too. My tail curls around my thigh and drapes over my cock. She watches the movement, and I preen as her gaze lingers on my lap.

When her head snaps up, she's once again blushing, and I find I quite enjoy bringing that pink tinge to her cheeks. She shifts and looks around the room. "Um. I really have to pee."

Of course. Having this little human around is going to take some getting used to. I scoop her into my arms, and she gasps. As I cross the room, I once again flick my fingers, and a door appears in the plaster wall. Striding into the newly added bathing chamber, I watch her eyes widen as she says, "You really can do just about anything with magic, can't you?"

I smile, leaning forward, letting a bit of dark mischief come into my eyes. "Oh yes, little sprite. Anything at all."

She squirms in my arms as she chews on her bottom lip, making my cock harden. She kicks her little feet as she says, "You can put me down."

I sit her on the toilet, and we stare at each other before she presses her thighs together, waving a hand. "Can you leave, please?"

"Why?"

"I'm not going to pee in front of you."

"This shouldn't matter. You are weak, and I will be here if you need me. Besides, I've dealt with your—"

She sticks her fingers in her ears, singing, "Lalalala. I don't need to hear about that."

When I grin down at her, she drops her hands with a cute frown. "At least turn around."

I oblige, waiting for the sound of her relieving herself to stop before I turn back to her. She presses her hands to her thighs, trying to stand, but I know she's not strong enough, so I lift her back into my arms. This is where she belongs. It makes me happy, and I realize it has been a very long time since I've felt that particular emotion.

I settle us back on the bed, and she once again pulls her shirt as far over her thighs as it will stretch as she asks, "So, your name?" When I don't respond, she lifts her face to look at me. "Unless it's like a power thing where you can't tell anyone your true name? I won't ask that of you. I—"

I wave her off. "It's nothing like that." I scratch the back of my neck, thinking. I'm sure I had a name at one point. Dropping my hand, I rest all four in my lap. "I can't seem to recall my name. Everyone just calls me, The Ancient, or, Ancient One." A little frown tugs at her lips, and she worries at the hem of her shirt once more. I can't be sure, but she seems sad. Slowly, I reach for her, and she allows me to run a single claw over her cheek. "It's just what happens with the passage of time. But if you want a name, Devana used to call me—"

"No!"

Fearing I somehow hurt her with my claws, I yank my hand back. She shakes her head, sending her fiery curls dancing around her face. "I don't care what that bitch ... witch ... goddess ... whatever, I don't care what she called you. She was the absolute worst."

Ana shudders as if she's shaking off the memory of the goddess., and I smile, realizing Devana *can* serve a purpose. My mate and I can commiserate on how much we both hate her.

"She was the worst, wasn't she?"

One corner of Ana's lips lifts in a half-smile, then a little chuckle bubbles up from her chest. She ducks her head, but her shoulders keep shaking. When she lifts her head again, there's a full-blown grin on her face, and her laughter fills the room. "She was the queen of awful."

I join in on her laughter. I can't stop staring at her bright eyes and the way her head cants to the left every time she laughs. As our chuckles die down, I clasp two of my hands as I wave a third. "Why don't you give me a name?"

Her mouth drops open, and she fiddles with the hem of her shirt again. "You want me to name you? That seems awfully personal."

"It is."

"Well, I, um ... I mean ..." She's cute when she

fumbles like this. I sit and wait, eager to hear what she comes up with. "Are you serious?"

I nod. "Or, you can just keep calling me, monster."

She taps her bottom lip. "No, no. But, Ancient One is really a mouthful."

You have no idea how much a mouthful I will be.

I shift my tail, attempting to hide my hardening cock as her gaze goes distant in thought. The idea of her giving me a name stirs something to life in my heart, and I find myself leaning forward in anticipation. After a few moments, she rubs her chest between her breasts. When she speaks again, instead of naming me, she says, "What makes you believe we are ... that we ..."

"That we are fated?"

She nods, not meeting my gaze. "I could smell it." I tap a claw to the golden thread stretched between us. "And, we are connected."

Her eyes search where I'm pointing. "You mean, literally?"

I nod. "I wish you could see it. The bond of fate is here, like a shining gold thread." I press a hand over my heart. "And it connects us here."

Her little hand clenches, bunching her shirt so it pulls it tight over her breasts. My nostrils flare as the faint scent of her arousal reaches me. My little sprite might be resistant, but there's a part of her that likes the idea of being bound to me.

She asks, "How do I know you're not just making this up?"

I smother the outrage that blooms through me. She doesn't understand. Lying about a mate bond is just not done. Ever. It's too sacred, a bond coveted by all.

I shake my head. "Why would I?"

"I don't know, but ..."

Two of my hands caress the sides of her face. Her eyes go wide, but she holds my gaze as I whisper, "I would not lie, not about this."

Shifting back, she moves out of my touch, and though it makes my fingers curl, I let her go. She tucks some of her hair behind her ear, dropping her gaze. "I believe *you* believe we are ... mates, but that kind of thing doesn't really happen. Soul mates aren't a thing."

"I assure you, it does, and they are." Turning, I point out the window. "Do you see that black castle there in the distance?"

She follows the direction of my finger. Her shoulders tense, then she forces a smirk as she turns back to me. "Yeah. I caught a glimpse of it when you threw me off the balcony." I wince, dropping my arm. She chuckles, but the sound is strained as she says, "I would have thrown Devana off the balcony too."

I take her hand, my thumb caressing her skin. She's trying to be brave, but I see the lingering trauma behind her eyes. The fact that she's sitting here talking to me, allowing me to touch her, is a miracle.

Keeping my voice low, I say, "But it was *you*, little sprite. It shouldn't have mattered that Devana's soul was inside you. I should have ... I should have listened to you."

She's silent for a long while, her hand resting in mine. I let her think, mentally building up a wall to dampen her rejection when it comes. When she looks at me, her face is serious. "Yes, you *should* have listened to me. But ... I kinda get it. Devana was a lying bitch. Roles reversed, I wouldn't have believed me. I think I would have done the same thing."

I don't deserve her.

She looks back over the valley. "Anyway, what about that castle?"

I let her redirect our conversation. I don't like talking about Devana either.

"A nepha lives there. The humans call them angels." She hums and squints as if she expects to see Malicious flying over his castle. "He found his fated mate in a human woman." She whips back around to face me, and I nod. "As did one of the Dremars." When her brow furrows, I add, "The large dark blue beings with horns and leathery wings. And an anza found their mate in a human male. A monster hunter at that."

She goes back to worrying the hem of her shirt with her free hand. "I ... this is all so ..."

Her hand slides out of mine, and I rub my fingers, trying to hold on to her warmth. She looks back towards Malicious' castle, then trails her gaze around the room. She settles and stares at the flames in the fireplace, her eyes going glassy. I wish I knew what she was thinking.

Shaking her head, she frowns, bites her lip, and curls her hands into fists. Her voice is low, but steady. "I know you said it was dangerous, but I don't recall it hurting at all when I was pulled here." *Interesting.* "And, ..." Her voice trails off, lowering as if she's speaking to herself. "I can't concentrate. My thoughts are all muddled." Her fists bunch in her shirt, and she raises her head, a determined glint in her eyes that has me concerned as she says, "Take me home."

Home? But this is her home. *I'm* her home. I apologized! She can't leave. We kissed. She was going to give me a name!

She wants to leave?

NO!

ANA

I don't want to leave.

I *need* to leave. I'm too confused. He wants me to name him for fuck's sake. And I was going to! I'm already in too deep. I can't think with his wintery scent everywhere and his rippling muscles doing things to my insides. Not to mention the glimpses I keep getting of his cock. I can't stop thinking about those fucking ruffles.

I need to leave. I don't belong here. It's a miracle I'm still alive. I need to get out while I can, while this ancient monster seems amicable—because who knows if he'll go back to trying to kill me?

You're his mate. He won't.

That's your aching pussy being optimistic.

And ...?

He hasn't answered me, but if his clenched hands are anything to go by, he doesn't like the idea of me leaving.

Am I truly trapped here? And why does that make my pussy clench?

"Little sprite, you are not yet strong enough."

"I think I am."

He shakes his head. "I am the better judge in this matter. You will stay here until I feel it is safe to take you across."

I try to sound outraged, but don't quite manage. "So, you're holding me hostage."

A rumbling sound comes from his chest, and his eyes turn a darker shade of red. "No, little sprite. I am keeping you safe."

"Take me home!" I battle against the tears threatening to close my throat. And what's even more frustrating is I'm not sure if I'm about to cry because he won't let me go, or out of fear that he will.

He narrows all his eyes at me, a wicked grin lifting his lips. I certainly don't swoon at that look as he waves a hand. A portal opens, shimmering like heat waves off hot pavement. Crossing his arms, he smirks. "There. Go ahead."

What?

I try to swallow the lump in my throat. He's ... he's letting me leave. Fine! Good. That's what I want. Shifting to the edge of the bed, I ignore my labored breaths. *What if he's right, though? What if it's terribly painful to cross The Divide back to my realm? What if it kills me?*

He just watches me with brows raised as if daring me to go. Fine!

I angrily push myself to my feet.

My legs crumple. Before I hit the stone floor, I'm back in his arms. The portal disappears as he lowers his head, his hair cascading over his shoulders and across my chest as he says, "I told you. You are not strong enough, but you still tried to leave me." He sounds angry, and it makes me want to press my thighs together and beg forgiveness.

One of his hands grips my chin, and by now the rough touch is familiar. I want to sink into it, but that only makes me angrier ... and hornier. He forces me to look at him. "Ana, understand. You are mine to care for. You are my mate. You aren't going anywhere."

He crushes his mouth to mine. His grip is bruising, and my lips tingle as he bites them. I try to hold on to the threadbare tendrils of my temper, and when I refuse to open for him, he growls. "Mine."

My fists slam into his chest, but he doesn't react. I can't do this. This is all too much. His lips crash back on mine, and fuck, he's such a good kisser.

Wait. No! Just because he thinks we are mates doesn't give him the right. My fingers wrap around his long silver strands, and I yank. The monster pulls back, and where I expect to see rage, there's only the fire of desire in his eyes. "You want to play that game, little sprite?"

One of his fists grabs my frizzy curls. I don't have time to brace, and my head falls back with his rough tug. My mouth opens on a whimper of pain that shoots pleasure throughout my body. He's there to swallow my weak protests, his tongue dancing with mine. I realize I'm kissing him back, and with another sharp pull on my hair, my back meets the rumpled blanket on the bed.

My hips rock up, and his hard cock presses against my thigh. Little fluttering movements tickle my skin, and I gasp. He breaks the kiss to bite at my ear. "You feel that, mate? My cock aches for you. My frills want to scrape your inner walls and tease your clit."

"Oh, fuck." I want that. But ... "Wait. Please. I just ... I need to think. I need to go hom—"

One of his hands bunches the shirt up under my

breasts, and another cups me between my thighs. I feel my wetness spreading across his palm, and even though I've pressed my lips tightly together, a moan escapes as a single claw flicks my clit.

He nips at my mouth. "If you say you want to leave me one more time, you'd better be prepared for the punishment, mate."

"I'm not your—"

A thick finger slides inside me, and I can't stop from clenching around him as he says, "Don't even think of finishing that sentence."

A second finger joins the first, stretching me. I try to plant my feet on the bed to get away from this intrusion, or to grind down harder. I'm not sure which. His fingers start pumping, and this time my moan is loud and wanton. He feels so damn good.

He sucks and nips along my throat before leaning back. Now's my chance to get out from under him. But with the next stroke of his fingers, I lift my hips to meet his hand. *Fuck. What am I doing?*

One of his other hands wraps around his cock, and I swallow as he strokes himself. The ruffles flutter and make little suction popping noises. "Do you see, little sprite? My frills will flick and grip your insides while the ones along the base will tease your ass and suck on your perfect cunt."

"Yes! Wait. No. Stop."

My pussy makes wet sounds as he drives his fingers deeper. "Hm. I don't think I will. And I don't think you want me to."

"I ..." His claw scrapes my inner walls, and I bow off the bed. "Fuck!"

"Yes, little mate."

"No, I mean ..." His tail slides between my thighs, up

my shirt between my breasts, then circles my neck. Shit. I'm so close. Just one orgasm, and then I'll make him take me home.

Yeah, right.

He strokes himself harder, and a clear viscous liquid begins to seep from those ruffles, coating his length. His hips thrust into his hand, and I can't help but imagine how good that would feel inside me.

He never stops pumping his fingers into my pussy, keeping a steady rhythm that's driving me higher towards my climax. His claw flicks my clit again, drawing a high-pitched gasp from my lips. When his tail tightens around my throat, I press the back of my head into the bed with a silent scream. I chase my pleasure, grinding on his hand.

"Yes, mate. You're so beautiful riding my fingers. Let me see you come."

I don't bother with an objection this time. This is my fantasy and real life all tangled together, so I grip his wrist with one hand and his tail with the other, demanding, "Harder."

His nostrils flare. His wet cock drips on my thigh as he curls his fingers with every pump inside me. "Yes, little sprite."

The pressure around my neck tightens, making the edges of my vision go fuzzy. I want to grab his horns and pull him to me for a kiss, but his tail holds me down. The pad of his finger rubs hard circles on my clit as the ones inside me scrape and press against my g-spot.

Another of his hands wraps around his balls and gathers the thick liquid pooling there. When he smears it on my pussy and clit, a warm tingling sensation intensifies the throbbing pulses inside me. I release his tail to use both hands to grip his wrist as I bear down on his hand. Sparks explode across my vision from both the pressure of his tail around my throat and the pleasure coursing from my core.

I try to scream as I come, but I can't. My body tenses, arching off the bed as much as his restrictive grip allows. I feel like I'm pulsing from head to toe. The waves die down, and I try to catch my breath, but then he growls, and his tail tightens even more. A second, and somehow stronger, orgasm chases the first. Or maybe this is just one long climax. I don't care. This is pure bliss. I'm floating in a sea of pleasure, each spasm crashing through me, causing me to clench over and over on his fingers.

As the pulses fade, wetness splashes my stomach. Looking down, I watch as the last of his release lands on me. His fangs have elongated, and the red fire in his eyes burns so brightly, they're rimmed in white.

A hoarse moan escapes my lips as he pulls his fingers out of me and his tail slides from around my neck. As soon as he sits back on his heels, looking all too pleased with himself, I shove backwards, pulling my shirt down.

It's hard to sound indignant while still riding the high of my powerful orgasm, but I try ... and fail when I cough before managing to get out, "That's it! Take me home! Now!"

He grins at me, holding up his wet fingers. He slides them into his mouth. I'm transfixed as he sucks on his fingers like he's trying to get every delicious drop of my release.

I shake my head. "No. Stop that. You're not being fair. You apologize, and then immediately pull a stunt like this?" I don't sound as mad as I meant to. In fact, I sound breathy and satisfied.

You are. And you want more.

Yes, please.

"Fair? I'd never play fair when it comes to my mate,

Ana. You're mine, so you might as well stop asking to go home. I wasn't going to let you go through that portal. I won't let you leave me."

Shifting to my knees, I sit up, still not eye level with him, but closer. The shift in position makes me dizzy, but after a few breaths, the room stops spinning. I point a finger in his face, ready to unleash my anger—both at him and at myself for being so turned on by his possessiveness.

He grabs my hand, easily wrapping his fingers all the way around my fist. He tugs, and I fall forward. Catching me, he places one hand on my lower back, another behind my neck, and the third on my hip. He presses my held hand to his chest, leaning down. Brushing a soft kiss against my lips, he whispers, "Please, don't ask me to let you go." He kisses me again, and my pussy has the audacity to clench with desire. "Please, Ana." He says my name like a prayer.

Fuck. He's really not playing fair at all.

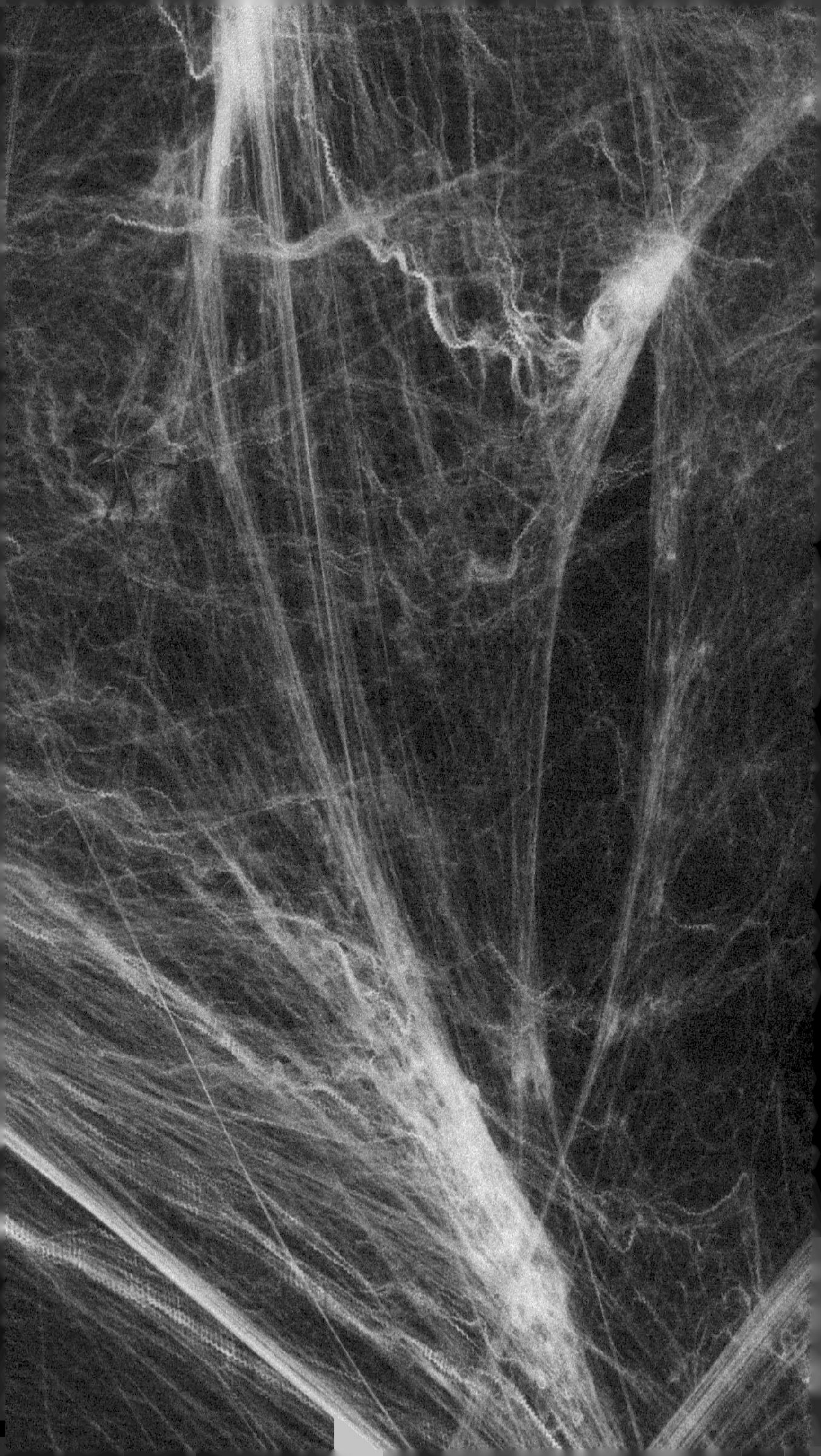

CHAPTER 18

THE ANCIENT

One taste of her pleasure, and I'm addicted. My mate isn't going anywhere. I wasn't lying. I will not play fair when it comes to her. I am a monster, after all.

Her monster.

I kiss her lips again, just to keep her taste on my tongue. Nibbling down her neck, I let my fangs scrape her skin, and I smile at her shiver. I whisper against her throat, "What is it back in your realm you are so eager to leave me for?"

I lick the soft skin where her neck meets her shoulder, and she moans, dropping her head farther to give me better access. Yes. Her body recognizes me. Her mate. She does too. She's just being stubborn. Which is fine. I've got time, and I know how to get my way. I always do.

Her small hands come to my chest as she says with a breathy voice, "That's distracting."

"Hmm. I know."

I chuckle as she squirms in my grip. I'm not sure if she meant to try to push away from me, but she ends up straddling my thigh instead. Perfect. Her cum smears across my leg, and I growl. Clamping my teeth against her flesh, I'm careful not to break the skin, but I do leave a mark. It's beautiful. Sitting back, I admire the red ring of flesh around her throat made by my tail. My finger marks are on her hips, and I want to lick them.

So, I do.

Scooping my hands under her ass, I lift her then flop her to her back once more. I'd keep her like this forever if I could. She squeaks in surprise, but the sound melts into one of pleasure as my long tongue laps at the red marks on her hips. Ana squirms, but I hold her in place as my tongue seeks the sweet heat between her thighs.

Just a taste.

My mate grips my horns, and with a voice deep and raspy from her pleasure, she says, "No, wait, I …"

I pause, smirking up her body. As a tease, my lips part, and I lick them, showing off my very long tongue. "What is it, little sprite?"

Her gaze remains on my mouth. She swallows, and I grin. Moving painfully slowly, I lower my head. My cock feels like it's swollen to the point of bursting, but all I want is her pleasure, her release, her … everything.

I unfurl my tongue, holding it above her pussy. Her breaths come in short pants, her red lips parted. She tugs on my horns, not to push me away, oh no. She pulls me closer.

I have every intention of letting my mate ride my face, but first …

Sitting back, I lament her touch as her hands fall from my horns. I hold her thighs open, my thumbs a mere inch from her cunt. My other hand wipes at my lips as my fourth hand slides up her stomach under the shirt. My fingers caress under her small breasts, teasing.

Taking my hand away from my mouth, I grip her chin, forcing her gaze to meet mine. "Well, little sprite? What is so important back there in your realm?"

She shifts, probably trying to get away from my touch, but I don't let her. I want the distraction to muddle her mind.

"Um ... my job."

"I believe you saw my hoard room. Money is of no concern."

"My apartment."

"My home is your home."

Her hand clings to my wrist that's holding her chin. "My friends. My life is back there."

"Wrong. Your life is with me. And my life is yours. And I think you know this. Does it not feel like your chest would rip in two if we were to be parted?"

Her other hand clenches at the shirt over her chest and she frowns. "No." I raise several brows, and she lowers her gaze. "Maybe. But I never said I was leaving you. I just want to go home ... for a bit. I can come back, right?"

"Would you? Willingly?"

She chews on her bottom lip, and I see her thinking. The longer her silence draws out, the angrier I get. And I'm not just angry. I'm nervous and frustrated and ... scared? I don't know if that's what I'm feeling. It's been too long since I've felt actual fear.

Emotions swirl in my gut to the point I want to lock her up. My claws lengthen with my growing panic, but my tone is even and steady. Deadly. "I've addressed all your concerns. You're staying."

Her brows furrow. "You're being unreasonable. This is all too fast."

"Reason has nothing to do with this."

She narrows her beautiful hazel eyes at me. "And let's not forget—"

I roll my eyes. "I tried to kill you ... several times. Yes, yes. I did say I was sorry. Have we not moved past that?"

She snorts that funny laugh of hers. "You're kidding, right?"

I shake my head, brushing my hand a little higher along her breasts. Her eyes widen, and her pupils dilate. I smile. She takes my breath away. I want to sink so deep inside her she feels me for several turns. I want to fuck her so hard, she can't walk. That's one way to keep my mate from leaving me.

I let my possessiveness bleed into my gravelly voice as I say, "You. Are. Mine."

Ana swallows but doesn't push back. Progress.

My thumbs stroke up and down the outside of her pussy, and her thighs flex under my grip. I scrape my claws across one small breast, curling my claw around her nipple, denying her the stinging touch she desires.

My mate arches into my touch, but I shake my head. "Name me, Ana. You'll need something to scream when I make you come again."

CHAPTER 19

ANA

Things have gone off the rails. I'm being pulled in different directions. My body, oh boy, my body wants to stay wrapped up in this monster and let him wring orgasms from me until I pass out.

Yeah, that sounds great.

But my mind ... Well, my mind also wants to stay, but it's whispering that I shouldn't *want* to stay. That I need to go back to my realm, to my home, away from this whole mess.

And a part of me wonders if I'm starting to buy into this whole mate thing because ... I want it. Sure, I want the orgasms and that fancy peen. But I also want the connection. I want what I've read about—that bond between two souls.

There must be *something* between us, otherwise, why does my chest ache when I think about leaving? Am I delusional? Have I gone crazy?

What's a girl to do?

His voice startles me from my thoughts. "I can actually see you thinking, little sprite. Surely, coming up with a name isn't that hard."

Oh yeah, I'm supposed to give this monster a name. Would *sex god* count? Because ... holy shit! And we haven't even had sex yet. *Yet.*

He continues, barely stroking my pussy, driving me mad. I know he knows *"he's being distracting."*

"Yes, I am. But can you blame me? My mate is just so tempting."

I flinch, once again not realizing I said that out loud. He chuckles, but he manages to make the sound seem dark and filled with promise as he palms my breast and squeezes. His thumbs barely slide inside me, only to pull my pussy lips apart, opening me to his hungry gaze as he says, "Name me, Ana."

Fuck! How am I supposed to think?

He hunted me from the moment I landed here. It was terrifying, but now, the thought of being hunted by him, desired, chased, fucked ...

"Vadasz." The name spills from me. He goes still, cocking his head to the side, all his red eyes blinking down at me as I whisper, "It's ... it's Hungarian for hunter. It seems appropri—"

"I love it."

And he sounds like he does. There's a reverence to his tone that wasn't there a moment ago, and a softness to his eyes that's making my insides melt. His large body curls over mine, and his lips brush tenderly across my mouth as he says, "My mate has gifted me the perfect name." He slicks his tongue into my mouth, and I can't stop my moan from rising. He makes that purring sound again. "Yes. I can't wait to hear my name coming from those lips as you come for me, Ana, my little sprite, my mate."

Jesus Christ. I'm about to come just from his words. Is that a thing?

Through the haze of desire, a thought pops into my head. *"Can monsters get humans pregnant?"*

He hums as two of his hands gently take my wrists, bringing them to the two horns I was gripping earlier. "Not unless you wanted it. My magic prevents my seed from taking hold." His hands tighten my grip on his horns. "But you just say the word."

I've never wanted kids. Still don't. But that was hot.

I bite my lip as his voice comes out all gravelly. "Hold on, little sprite. Ride my face. Cover my mouth with your cum. I want to feast on you and erase all thoughts of your realm. I am your home now."

Oh yeah, I'm supposed to be trying to get him to take me home. But ...

Ride him! Get yours! He says you're mates. That doesn't just mean you are his ... he is yours. Take him.

Well, I've convinced myself.

Using his horns, I push him between my thighs. His grin lights me up. He holds my gaze as two hands grip my hips and the other two continue to hold me open. Having multiple hands sure does come in, well, handy.

Internally, I chuckle at myself, then all humor flies out the window as his tongue spears inside me. I buck off the bed as much as his grip allows. He eats me like I'm his last meal, and when he growls against my pussy, I feel the vibrations all the way to the top of my head. Even my hair follicles tingle.

I hold on to his horns for dear life, chasing my orgasm that's building ... fast. Using his horns as leverage, I grind onto his face, uncaring if he can breathe. He's a monster with magic and crazy powers. He'll figure it out.

His hands are everywhere, touching, stroking, caressing ... His tongue spears inside me again and again, going so deep, I feel the tip curling and flicking against my inner walls. It's heaven. I'm so close. It's torture.

He growls again, and my pussy clenches as I thrust my hips against his mouth. The moment he sucks my clit, I explode.

"Asz!" I scream the nickname into the firelit room, the sound bouncing off the stone walls.

He keeps sucking as his teeth scrape and his tongue flicks. I fall apart, unable to put myself back together. It's too much. I'm swollen, and sensitive, but he doesn't stop. I yank on his horns, but he doesn't budge from between my thighs. The sight of him there, his head buried in my pussy, all his eyes closed in pleasure ... it nearly rips another orgasm from me. This powerful monster is ... "mine."

His eyes snap open, and he lifts his head. His lips glisten with my release, and he licks some away as he says, "Yes, Ana. Yours."

"Vadasz, I—"

The room spins, and when I settle, I find myself in his lap, his arms surrounding me, petting me, stroking my hair. It tickles slightly as he nuzzles my head, but then he says, "I know. I know. You want to go home."

"No! What? Wait. I mean ... what?"

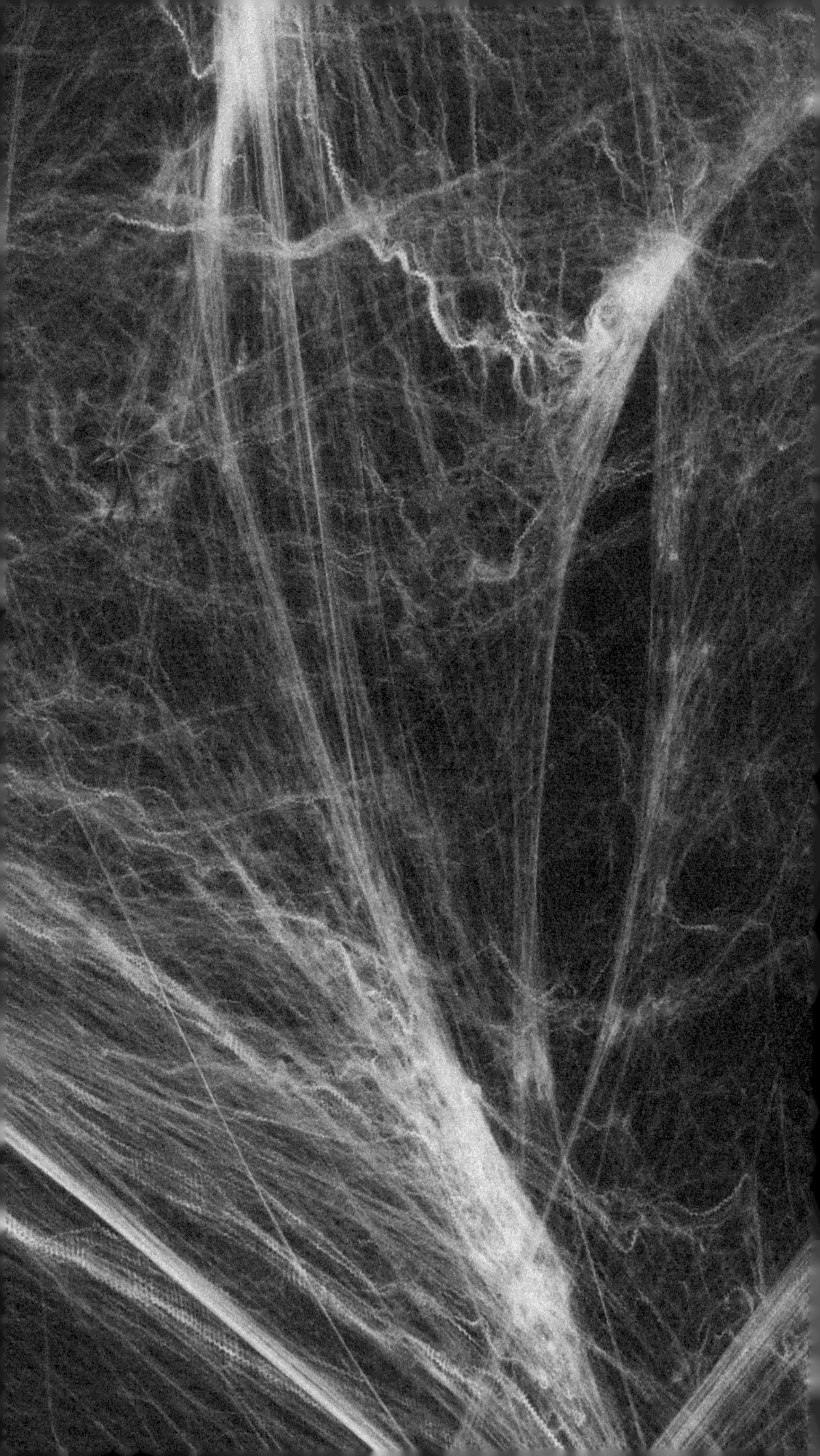

CHAPTER 20

VADASZ

I keep myself from releasing the chuckle in my throat. Once again, I don't think she realizes she said that out loud. My poor little mate is conflicted. That's good.

She nibbles on her lower lip, and I recall how she screamed my new name during her climax, and I don't think I've experienced a more perfect moment in all my years.

Her eyes close as I continue to comb my fingers through her hair, careful not to tug when they get snared in the tangles. She smiles, melting into my touch. "I know what you're doing."

"And what is that, little sprite?"

"You're using your magic hands to distract me."

I kiss the sensitive spot behind her ear, earning me a delightful shiver. "Magic hands, huh?" I continue to comb her long hair as my other hands massage her neck, shoulders and back. Her sigh brings a satisfied grin to my face. "Is it working?"

Her voice is low, edging towards sleepy. "You know it is." In a matter of seconds, her breath evens out, and her body goes lax. My mate is asleep in my arms, flushed and warm from the pleasure I gave her.

I shift, ready to curl around my mate and rest while she sleeps, but then her stomach grumbles. Shit. All she's had in the past seven turns—no, eight now—is a small bowl of broth and some water I forced down her throat. My gaze travels over her face, just now noting the dark circles under her eyes. She needs rest, but she also needs to eat.

"Ana."

She gives me no reaction, so I brush my hand over her cheek. "Ana. I know you're tired, but you must eat."

Still nothing, and now my heart is beating too fast. I gently shake her, and her head lolls over my arm. Fuck. She's passed out ... again. I fed her pleasure instead of food, forgetting how fragile humans are.

Fuck. Fuck. Fuck.

I'm about to push my magic into her mind once more to force her awake, but she groans softly, and her eyes blink open. "Oops. Think I fell asleep." A sweet smile lifts her cheeks. "It was those magic hands."

Relief punches through me so swiftly, I have to concentrate to keep from puncturing her skin with my claws. "And you will sleep more, but first, you must eat something."

Her stomach gurgles again, and she presses her palm over it. "Yeah. I am pretty hungry."

"What would you like?"

"Everything I can think of sounds amazing, but I'm

not sure what I can actually handle. I don't want to make myself throw up."

I have no knowledge of what a weak human should eat. I only guessed to feed her broth before because that's what grateslung eat when they are weak from magic depletion. But soup doesn't seem like enough.

Uncertainty flutters through me. I should take her back to the human realm and let the healers there take care of her. But I won't. So ... this needs to be done. I shift, setting my mate on the bed before standing. "Stay. Rest. I'll return quickly."

I'm turning to walk through a portal when her voice stops me. "Wait! Please don't lock me in here aga—"

A thud and a cry of pain has me spinning back around. Ana lays sprawled on the floor, her shirt once again bunched up high around her thighs. Who would have guessed a simple shirt would be so distracting? Getting her hands under her, she tries to push herself up, but her body shakes with the effort.

I have her bundled in my arms the next moment, and I carefully tuck her into the blankets. "Stop, little sprite. You are too weak. I won't lock you in, I promise. I just need you to stay here for me, okay?" She falls back into the pillows, closing her eyes and pressing a palm to her head. I reach for her, my hands hovering, unsure what to do for my mate. "Are you alright? Are you injured?"

She shakes her head, but quickly stops. "I'm dizzy. I'm ... I don't ..."

Her words are slurring, and her hand falls to the bed as if even holding it to her head was too much effort. I stroke her hair, pressing a kiss to her head, not liking how labored her breaths are. "Rest. I won't be gone long." When she cracks open an eye and opens her mouth, I don't let her argue. "Please, Ana."

With a sigh, she closes her eyes again and relaxes. I don't think she'll try to leave again ... Regardless, she's not strong enough. Still, I wrap my magic around her, around the bed, and around the room. I'll know if she moves a single toe.

She's asleep again, so I kiss her once more before tearing myself from her side. I rush through a portal and grimace at the room I enter. The black marble floor reflects my dark image. The black walls seem to absorb the light of the sconces, and I sneer at my reflection in the black-gilded mirror leaning against the far wall.

In contrast to this gothic room, the gold nepha before me is like a spotlight, and I know this is intentional. Malicious is a vain creature. The human female riding his cock shrieks in surprise, almost tumbling off their bed if not for Malicious' grip on her waist. With a flex of his golden skin, the nepha flips so his mate is under him, his metallic bronze wings spread to hide her naked form. Not that he should be concerned. I only have eyes for my little sprite.

Malicious looks at me over his shoulder, and I see the anger and annoyance in his eyes, but his voice is calm as he says, "What can I do for you, Ancient One?"

I jerk my head towards the female trying to peek at me between Malicious' metal feathers. "I actually need to speak to your mate."

The nepha dares to growl at me, and I realize he's still inside her when I hear the wet slide of his cock leaving her body. She shivers, and her eyes roll back. I smirk as Malicious turns to face me. Shifting off the bed, he stands, spreading his wings to shield his mate. With hands on hips, he looks up to meet my gaze. "No."

"No?" My form expands, smoke peeling away from skin as my eyes burn white. My tail thrashes in anger. He's delaying me. Every second away from Ana is a second too long. At least my magic is telling me she hasn't moved, and the faint pulse of the bond thread suggests she's still sleeping.

A sun-kissed hand pushes through the nepha's wings, landing on his hip. "Mal, let him ask his question."

His shoulders are tense, and even though his cock is still hard and wet from being in his mate just moments before, he doesn't move. "Ask."

I pause, unsure how much to reveal. But then I realize it doesn't matter. My mate needs help, and I don't know what to do.

"I've found my mate. She's human."

Malicious' lips quirk with a smug smile that I want to punch off his face, but his female gasps and scoots to the edge of the bed. Her feet poke over the side and she moves to stand, but Malicious reaches back, holding her behind him. "Summer, my love, you're still naked."

I roll all my eyes in impatience. Who cares who is bare or not? With a flick of my hand, I clothe the female, and she giggles. I talk over her sounds of surprise. "There was an ... incident that caused my mate to remain unconscious for seven turns. She drank some water and some broth, but she's weak and hungry and I don't know what she needs."

Malicious crosses his arms with a grin. "Well, well, well."

The humans may call his kind angels, but he looks like a demon right now, and I'm tempted to fling him across the room. But his female stands and pushes around his wings. "Mal, stop it."

When he looks down at her, his face softens as I've felt mine do when I look at Ana. His voice is soft as he says, "It's just nice to know the all-powerful Ancient One doesn't know everything. And now he has a mate. A human mate!" His gaze slides back to me, and I clench my fists. "He's about to learn how little power he has when it comes to a human woman who holds his heart."

He speaks the truth, but I'm tired of hearing him talk. He's not giving me answers, and as such, is in the way. My magic rams into Malicious, and he rocks back on his heels as I push him across the room, holding him against the wall.

His mate watches with wide eyes, her gaze flicking between me and her captured mate. When Malicious flexes, trying to break my hold, she bites her lip and tilts her head at me. "Can you keep him like that after you leave?"

Malicious barks, "Summer!"

She blushes, tucking her short hair behind her ear. "Just for like, twenty minutes. Maybe thirty."

A smirk pulls at my lips. I like this petite female. "Gladly. Just tell me what I need to know."

All playfulness slides from her face as she taps her bottom lip in thought. "You said she drank some water and some broth. And she kept it down?" I nod. "I'm not a medical professional, but I think it's safe to let her try to drink juice for the vitamins and sugars, and rice or mashed potatoes should be okay to eat. Stick with plain food. Take it slow." She points a finger at me, her gaze dipping to my cock before coming right back to my face. "And I don't just mean the food."

Malicious chuckles, but his little mate crosses her arms. "I'm serious. Don't push her." A little smirk curls her lips. "Patience is a virtue."

I grimace. "Not in the monster realm."

"Well, you're mated to a human." She shifts her weight to one hip. "In fact, maybe I should go with you to—"

"No." Malicious and I both bark out the word.

She frowns. "Well, fine. Just take it slow."

Malicious huffs a laugh, and I tighten his restraints as I say, "I'll ... try." Turning to go back through my portal, I say, "Thank you, Summer." I glance at Malicious and grin. "And enjoy. He won't be able to move from that spot for, what did you say, thirty minutes?"

Malicious strains against my magic, and I chuckle, but his mate nods, her attention fully on him as she says, "Thanks, and good luck. Let us know if you need anything else, and I can't wait to meet her."

I watch Summer stalk across the bedroom, and with a flick of my magic, her clothes are gone. Malicious growls, but to his credit, keeps his mouth shut, his eyes on his mate. Their skin is a bright contrast to their black surroundings. It's quite beautiful. Then she reaches for his cock, her lips parted.

Malicious curls a wing around her and growls again, keeping his hungry gaze on the woman before him as he says, "You can go now, Ancient One. Your mate is waiting."

I tear my attention from the couple. He's right. My little sprite is waiting. As I stride through the portal, I say, "My name is Vadasz."

I catch his stunned expression as I close the portal.

CHAPTER 21

ANA

The scent of cinnamon pulls me from my dreamless sleep.

I'm not sure how many turns it's been, but if I were to count the number of shirts Vadasz has created for me ... today would be the seventh day since I woke up after the whole goddess thing. That means I've spent two weeks here in the monster realm.

How time flies when you're falling in love.

I roll over, stretching against the soft blanket, my head sinking into the pillow. I feel much better. Sitting up, today's new shirt lays cool against my skin. The green silk is light, and my nipples pebble against the fabric. Vadasz always dresses me in a long shirt. Nothing else. The silent flames in the fireplace keep me warm, and when we're not in this room, the heat of his body does the job just fine.

I can't keep the smile from my face as the air shimmers in the way I've learned proceeds his arrival through one of his portals. The glow of his red eyes appears first, and a second later, he steps through. As always, my gaze lands on his cock first, still craving to find out what those frills would feel like inside me.

My chest tightens with the ache of doubt. He hasn't touched me like *that* since that first time, and I don't know why.

The tray he has balanced on one hand draws my attention. Pastries covered in dripping frosting sit on a plate, the surgery scent making my mouth water. My eyes catch on the burst of color in a little bowl. Cubed fruit, perfectly ripe. A tall glass of water barely sways with his easy gate, and steam dances from a mug of spiced cardamom, ginger, and honey tea—a drink he makes me every "morning" since he found out it's my favorite way to start the "day."

Well, besides ...

My cheeks flush, and I shift, smoothing the blanket as a distraction.

"Good morning, little sprite. What would you like to do this turn?"

I have a few ideas that involve us staying in bed for most of the day, but I say, "Let's just see where the day takes us."

He nods, and as he settles the tray on the bed, my thoughts go over the past week.

He has hand fed me every meal, and snacks in between. Each offering gets a little more decedent, and I've regained the weight I lost ... plus some.

The second day after I woke, he took me on a tour through his seemingly endless mountain home. As we strolled, hands occasionally brushing, I told him about my job running the garden center, and how I love to spend as much time as I can in the tropical species room. Those plants are temperamental and fickle but reward you with the most amazing blooms.

He took my arm when he noticed I was getting tired, offering to return me to *our* bed so I could rest. The way he said "our bed" made me swoon, but I was enjoying our conversation. I wanted more ... more of him. Whatever he'd give me. So, with an indulgent smile, he took a little more of my weight against his arm, and we kept walking.

He regaled me with stories about a realm that is ninety percent plant life, and how the beings that live there survive off photosynthesis. Their skin is green, and they root into the earth to commune with their planet.

I wonder if he'll take me there one day? I do miss the sun. I miss the heat on my skin and the colors it paints the sky as it welcomes and bids farewell to the day. And I miss my plants.

The next day, we were in the thermal pools, and as he washed my hair, I shared the story of how I learned to swim as a child, teaching myself at a nearby lake. I'd wade in to the shallow end, trying to copy the others I'd seen swimming. I'd keep myself afloat for longer stretches until I could swim all the way across.

I shiver as I recall him leaning over, whispering in my ear that I was brave, and I realized no one had ever called me that before. It was nice.

As he rinsed my hair, he told me he didn't remember how he learned to swim, but he shared a story about a stretch of time he spent in my realm as a serpent. He'd found a lovely cool lake shrouded in mist and decided to stay a while. He smiled wistfully as he told me about the occasional human that would wander too close, affording him a snack. I'd acted shocked, but couldn't help but laugh. When I asked where this was, he couldn't recall, but when he described the area, my mouth dropped open as I said, "You? You were the loch ness monster?" He'd looked confused, having never heard the term, and that made me clutch my stomach in laughter. I had to kick my feet to keep from dipping under the water.

And two days ago, we spent time strolling along the dirt paths through the woods of the valley—the same woods where he hunted me. But this time, I felt safe as I marveled at the beauty and stillness of it all. He said it was so quiet because nothing dares disturb him. I think he was testing me, to see if I was still afraid, and reminding me I probably should be. But I wasn't. I'm not. And to prove it, I interlaced my fingers with his. He blinked down at our hands for a few strides before the claw of his thumb gently scraped back and forth across my skin. It was sweet.

It was then I realized I was falling for him.

So, yeah, it's been two weeks, and he hasn't taken me back home.

And I haven't brought it up. I've let it go, for now. Instead, I'm focused on learning about my monster, because after every interaction, I find I want more.

Mates. Dare I hope this is real?

The mattress dips, bringing me out of my thoughts as he sits next to me. I clasp my hands in my lap, waiting. He's made it very clear he enjoys feeding me, and I must say, I enjoy it too.

He spears a piece of orangey-pink fruit with a claw. *What is it about being hand fed that's so erotic?* When I open my mouth, he leans in. Sliding the sweet fruit into my mouth, he whispers against my cheek, "I can smell your desire, little sprite. It is sweeter than any treat on this tray."

"*Oh, fuck.*"

He chuckles.

Why can't I keep my thoughts inside where they belong?

The fork looks like a doll's toy in his hand as he cuts and spears what looks like a piece of cinnamon roll. He brings it to my mouth, and I slowly wrap my lips around it, holding his gaze. The red in his eyes flickers with a tinge of white at the edges, and it's only with great willpower that I keep my eyes from dropping to his cock. I swallow down the sticky bun, and another forkful of the pastry approaches me. I find I'm not hungry—for food anyway—but I take it, just for something to do besides jump him.

Bite by bite, he feeds me, handing me the water every so often. Once the food is gone, he puts the magically hot cup of tea in my hands, then shifts and moves behind me. I'm bracketed by his strong thighs as his fingers run through my hair.

This is also something he has done every day—play with my hair.

Vadasz gathers a small section and begins to braid. It's such a domestic action, his touch is so tender, and all I can think about is the fact that I could shift back just a little to feel his length against my back.

I take a sip of tea, inhaling the combined spiciness of the cardamon and ginger balanced with the sweet honey, trying to ease the stiffness in my spine. He must notice my tension, because he asks, "What is it, Ana?"

I'm glad he's behind me so I don't have to look at his face as I say, "You haven't ... I mean ... I just thought ... before, you were so ..."

Damn it, get out a complete sentence Ana.

Vadasz stops the movement of his fingers, leaning into me. He's hard, and the frills along his length grab and suck at the material of my shirt as he says, "Never in all my life have I struggled with patience as I have these past few turns."

A tiny bit of tea splashes over the rim of my cup, dotting my shirt. My voice comes out low and breathy. "Then why ...?"

There's a long pause, and I think he won't answer, but then his fingers start twining through my hair again, and he says, "Malicious' human told me I needed to be careful with you ... to be patient."

"And you listened?" I don't mean to sound so shocked, and his hands go still once more. Setting the cup on the tray, I turn, shifting onto my knees. I can't read the expression in his eyes, but I know what I said and the way I said it might be hurtful. I smile softly, rising to kneeling so I can press my hand to his jaw. "Sorry. Just, the thought of *The Ancient One* following the advice of a lowly human ..."

His head leans into my touch. "Humans aren't lowly. At least, you aren't." His many eyes search my face, and one of his hands brushes my hair over my shoulder.

Okay Ana, time to be bold.

Keeping my hand on his face, I trail the other down his chest. His eyes widen before they narrow, the fire in them flickering. His lips part, and that soothing purring sound vibrates under my touch.

Lower and lower, I brush my fingers over the v of his hip, and then I feel it—a fluttering against my skin. Finally!

His cock is even darker than the rest of him, and the contrast of our skin is ... beautiful.

Little sucking pulls pop along my hand, and of course I can't help but imagine how amazing it would feel inside me and on my clit. I wrap my hand around him, and he growls. My thumb and middle finger meet, but just barely, as I stroke him. A moan builds in my throat as his frills flutter and suck at my skin. My palm grows wet as those ruffles release their lubricant. My grip glides over him. I watch in awe as the frills dance around my fingers with every stroke. Such a strange and wickedly delightful sensation—like sentient lace ... with suction cups.

I'm broken from my trance as one of his hands wraps around mine. For a moment, I hold my breath, ready for him to guide me to stroke him as he likes. Instead, he stops me. I lift my head to meet his intense gaze.

Testing him, I slide my hand up the length of his cock, and he lets me, his hand moving with mine. I grin, ready to unleash my monster. "Your mate needs you, Asz."

He growls, deeper than I've heard before, and his muscles tense, but I move before he does. Still holding his cock, I scoot forward to straddle him, sending the plate and cup on the tray rattling. Vadasz doesn't break my gaze, but one of his hands twitches, and the tray and its contents disappear.

I take that as a green light, so, using my free hand, I grip the hem of my silk shirt and bring it over my head, reluctantly letting him go to discard my only piece of clothing. As my shirt floats to the floor, I bring my hand to my lips and lick the lubrication.

His hand grips my hip, squeezing.

The taste of him is salty and clean, like an ocean breeze. I lick again, and his nostrils flare. He opens his mouth to speak, but I move, silencing him. Rising, I grip his cock as my legs squeeze his hips. I line him up, rubbing his tip over my sensitive clit and between my pussy lips. His other hands land on my body, his claws digging in slightly.

The need to feel his frills inside me is an obsession.

With one slow movement, I slide down his length.

My mouth drops open, and my head falls back as he stretches me. He's so big. It burns, but those ruffles ... they caress me, stroking every available inch. My entire body is one pulsing heartbeat. My pussy throbs. I keep going until he's completely buried in me. The second he bottoms out, the frills at his base tickle my ass and latch onto my clit, sucking and pulling.

My orgasm hits me hard. Pleasure rolls through me. It's violent. It's electric. For a moment, I think I've closed my eyes, but no, my vision has blacked out, sparking stars dancing at the edges.

And then he moves.

His hands easily lift me, and when he shoves me back down his length, he bucks his hips. Wetness drips between us as I grind down on him. Two of his hands pinch my nipples, and I gasp, "Thank god for a mate with four hands."

He chuckles, the sound dark and full of promise. "Four isn't enough. I need to touch all of you, Ana."

Another hand grabs my ass, and another collars my throat. Yet another gathers my hair at my nape and tugs, while a seventh, or is this the eighth, teases my back hole. His tail wraps around my calf, and I do what I wanted to do that first time. Reaching up, I grab his horns and pull him to me.

Our lips crash together, tongues tangling, teeth biting. The sound of our bodies coming together is loud and messy ... and so erotic.

I may be on top, but he's dominating me, moving my body, fucking up into me.

I'm so close.

He slows, and I whine, but his kisses turn tender. He sips and licks at my mouth. His thrusts are leisurely, and his hips roll every time he bottoms out. When his frills suck and pop against my clit again, I moan into his mouth. "Please, Asz. I'm so close."

"Say it again."

I know what he wants. He's obsessed with his name.

And I'm obsessed with him. My monster.

"Asz."

He snaps his hips a little harder. "Again."

"Asz."

His lips trail down to the base of my neck where it meets my shoulder, his teeth scraping. "Again."

Pain spikes as his fangs break my skin, but then he starts sucking. I scream with pleasure as I bounce on his cock, blissed out by the fluttering popping of his frills. Every pull of his lips on my neck sends a shock right through my clit.

For a second, a gold thread shimmers between us, but when I blink, it's gone. And then his hand tightens around my throat, right over my pulse points.

"Asz! Oh, yes! Yes!"

His voice is guttural and gravelly as he drives his cock into me. "Mine."

"Yes! Yours. Yours, Asz!" I burst apart. My vision blurs, and tears fall down my cheeks. Pulsing pleasure rips through me. My mate grunts and growls, and I feel him holding back.

No. Not with me. I swallow to clear my throat. "Asz. Please. I want your cum. Fill me until I'm dripping."

His lips tear away from my neck, his hips stilling. His eyes shimmer with emotion, then he releases a growl mixed with a groan as he drives into me. He throws his head back, and I'm transfixed as his silver hair floats around his head and horns, his fangs bared, slightly red from my blood. His eyes burn. They burn for me.

Another wave of ecstasy punches through me.

A finger, or maybe it's his tail, wet with his secretions, pushes at my back hole, sliding in slightly. We both groan. It feels so good. I'm so full. He's everywhere, and I want more. I *need* ... "More." I bear down on an exhale, and whatever is back there slides farther into my ass. I gasp at the pleasure-pain.

Despite having just come, he's still hard inside me, still thrusting. His grip around my throat is gentler, but still directs my body, as do his many other hands. His voice is soft, almost reverent like a prayer as he says, "Ana. My Ana."

My eyes nearly bug out of my head as his entire body expands and grows larger. Smoke leaks from his skin. I scream, trying to escape the pain of his next thrust. He's too big, and getting bigger.

"I ... I can't. You're too much. Oh, god. Asz!"

My ass and pussy stretch to the point of tearing. It hurts. It feels amazing. My hands look tiny as they fall to his massive chest, feeling the vibrations of his purr.

He says, "You can take it, mate. You were made for me. Look how well your body takes me, little sprite."

And I do. My gaze drops to where our bodies are joined. We are drenched with our combined cum and the lubrication seeping from his frills. Between his thrusts, I catch the sight of his fingers pumping into my ass. Yes, fingers, plural. Large ones. Two of them.

He groans, "So beautiful."

It's not. It's carnal. It's messy. It's fucking sexy. "Yes."

My back hits the mattress, and he looms over me. He's so huge, all I see is him. His hips snap forward, driving me into the mattress. The wood feet of the bed screech over the floor with each of his thrusts until the headboard hits the wall with a rhythmic, *thump thump thump*. I try to wrap my legs around him, but he's too broad. One of his hands, or maybe it's a new one, grips my thigh holding me wide.

He fucks me. Hard. Just how I've always fantasized. My monster.

He roars as he comes again. The sound is so primal, it tips me over the edge into yet another climax. He keeps thrusting, grinding, alternating between hard and demanding, and slow and intentional. I come again, and again, and again, until the blackness at the edges of my vision takes over completely. A thought floats through my head ...

Am I about to pass out from too many orgasms? Just one more thing from my books I didn't think was real.

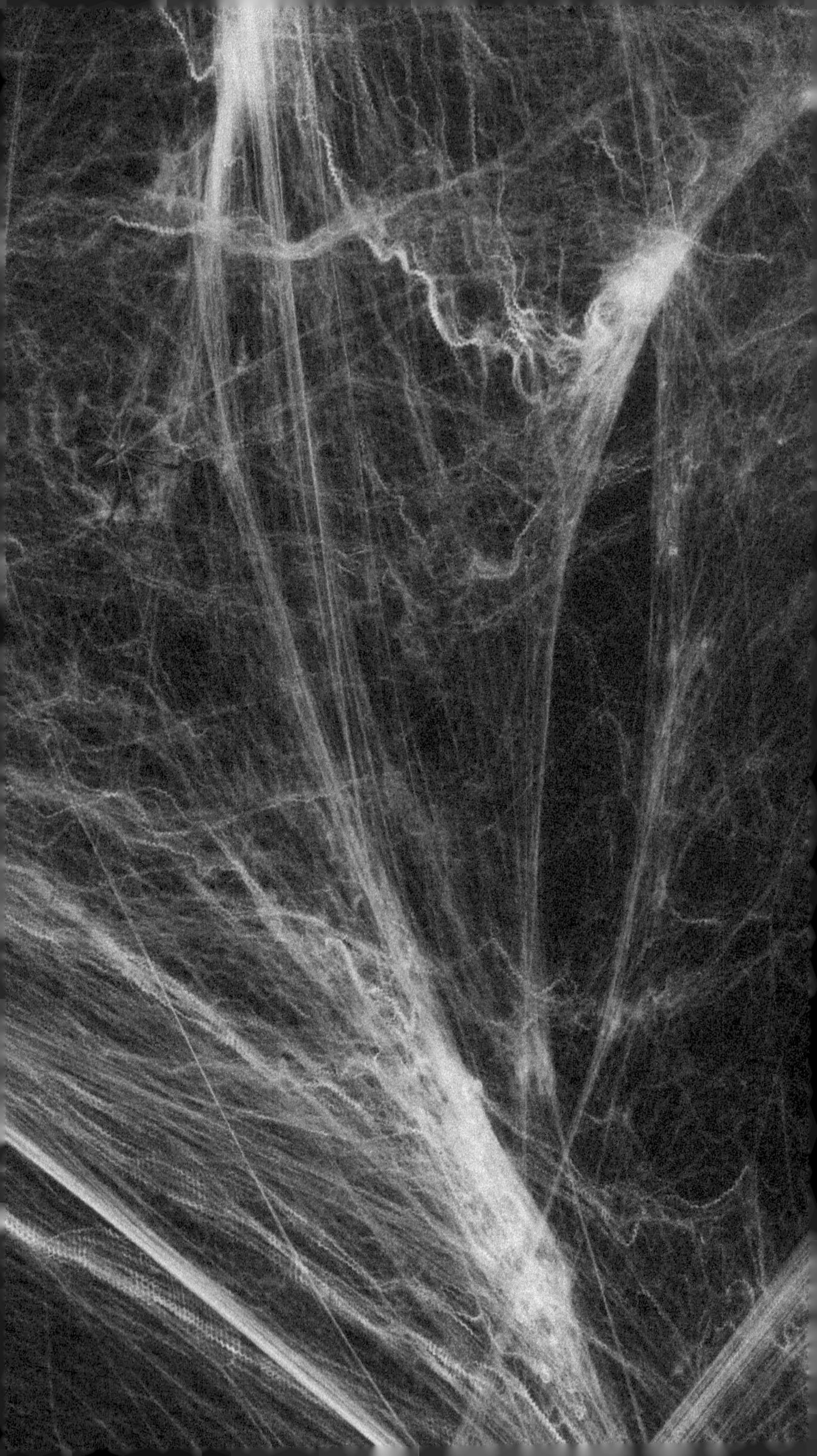

CHAPTER 22

VADASZ

I claimed her. I bit her. I didn't ask. I didn't explain. I just took what was mine.

She is mine ... but she has no idea what that really means.

Or maybe she does. She did say she'd read about fated mate bonds in her books. Though, how accurate can they be?

Instead of taking her to the thermal pools to clean us, I open a portal, hugging my sleeping mate against my chest. She smells like sex, like me, but her apple and honey scent is still there, soothing me. Ana is everything.

Striding through the portal, I grit my teeth against my unease. The room is small and tidy. Plants adorn almost every surface, and I smile at the large carnivorous one sitting on a shelf with some type of machine that spews up puffing vapor clouds. But several of the plants around the room have wilted blooms and yellow leaves.

This won't do.

With a little push of my magic, I energize the plants, even coaxing a few new blooms to unfurl. When I turn to take in more of the space, my horns scrape the ceiling, so I make myself smaller—too small for my liking.

I take a slow breath, trying to ease the tightness in my chest. Nope. I still don't like the human realm. It stinks. The air is dirty, and it's very loud, even during the times humans are supposed to be sleeping. Their electricity hums and crackles all the time. Their vehicles rumble. Even the sky isn't safe from them, with their planes criss-crossing almost constantly.

Ana stirs, nuzzling into me. I'm not sure what to do, so I just stand in the middle of the room as she yawns and opens her eyes. "Asz?"

"I'm here, little sprite."

She looks up into my face, and for a moment, I fool myself into believing there's love in her gaze. But she stiffens and looks around. "Wha—?"

I've dreaded bringing her here, but I must admit, as the morning sun touches her face, lighting her up in golds and reds, I know this moment alone was worth it. She's stunning. She was made to be lit by the sun—any sun, in any realm. She's not meant for the darkness of my world.

Still, I won't let her go.

"Asz? Why are we in my apartment? How did you even find it?"

"It's easy enough to trace your scent."

She shifts, and I set her down. Her head swivels as she looks around, but then she spins, grabbing my arms. "It's morning!" I nod, unsure why she seems so panicked. "The Divide. It's up. How are you ...? Isn't it painful? Is this draining you?" She tugs on me, and my chest swells.

"Let's go. Oh my god! The blood carvings! How did you get past them? I—"

"Ana." She looks up at me, her wide eyes searching my face then my body for any sign of injury or discomfort. Fuck, I love her. "Ana, I'm fine. I am—"

"An Ancient." She relaxes with a smile, rising to her toes, lips seeking. Pulled to her like a moon to its planet, I lean over, pressing my mouth to hers. The kiss is soft, sweet, and too quick.

Lowering her heels back to the floor with a little thud, my mate turns and walks across the room in a few strides, her fingers trailing over the leaves of her plants. "They're still alive. In fact, they're thriving." Glancing at me over her shoulder, she narrows her eyes at me. I shrug, and she smiles, "Thank you."

Once she reaches the window, she stops, looking over the rooftops and the lazy, pink-tinged clouds crawling across the sky. It's a picture-perfect moment. With the soft light streaming through the window, I can see every curve of her perfect body through her shirt. Her long hair curls down her back, cast in golds and dark reds, and the toes of her bare feet curl into the rug as if she's re-familiarizing herself with her space.

Slowly, she turns around, and I don't think my heart has ever beat this hard. She fidgets in place, shifting her weight from foot to foot, making her shirt sway against her thighs. "Thank you, Vadasz, for bringing me here."

I don't answer because I'm not sure what to say. This isn't what I expected. I thought she would shriek and laugh and run around, happy to be back in her home. I expected to become an afterthought. I came here ready to drag an angry Ana back to my mountain once she'd gathered what she wanted from this place.

But she has barely taken her eyes off me.

When I remain silent, she takes a step forward, and the light haloes her as she says, "I can see it, you know."

I blink several times. "See what, little sprite?"

A smirk plays at her lips. "The thread." My eyes widen as she reaches for her neck. Her touch plays over the mark I left on her skin. "You bit me. I saw it, but then it disappeared. But now ..." She looks at the bright gold thread stretched between us. Her hand leaves her neck, and her fingers dance along the bond. The sensation makes me shiver, and my cock starts to rise. "It's beautiful." Her eyes slowly lift to meet mine, and my lips part as she says, "You're beautiful."

I think I need to prostrate myself at the feet of the Fates. I was very, very wrong to doubt them.

She takes another step, her finger trailing along the thread. I feel her touch brush against my soul. A few more steps bring her before me. Her head tilts back, exposing the long column of her neck. My mouth waters, but I promised myself I'd give her time in the human realm.

Patience. I can do this. For her.

Her warm palm lands on my chest. "Asz, take me home."

Confusion stalls me for a moment, but when she doesn't break my gaze, I growl, wrapping my arms around her back and under her ass to lift her. She presses her lips to mine, her hand cupping my cheeks. My insides melt. My muscles tense. My body burns for her.

I wrap us in my magic, not bothering to ask what she needs or wants. I grab it all. The moonlight spills through the open balcony doors of our bedroom, the silent flames dancing and flickering in the fireplace. My tongue slips between her lips, and she licks me. My cock jerks, and my frills vibrate. "Ana."

I walk us towards the balcony, being careful to step

around all her plants, her few pieces of furniture, her clothes, knickknacks, rugs, and even her dishes and silverware ... all haphazardly placed around the bedroom.

She giggles, and I pause to take in her joyful smile as she says, "You brought everything? I can't believe my entire apartment fits in this room."

"I will help you find a place for it all. Anywhere you want. You can have your own room if that's what you desire. For your things. Not you. You sleep here, with me. Always."

"Always."

She has stollen my breath and my heart. Everything I am, being belongs to her.

A chilly breeze plays with our hair as I step outside. I wrap her in my magic like a blanket, and my fingers thread through her hair. The moonlight removes the gold from her strands, painting them a cooler shade. Darker, but no less beautiful. "You were made for sunlight, Ana."

She copies me, stroking my silver hair. "You were made for starlight." Tilting her head, she smiles at me. "And isn't that just perfect? The sun and the stars."

I frown. "But their light cannot exist at the same time." I kiss her with a sad smile. "The sun is too bright. Your brilliance is blinding."

Her arms wrap around my neck, her fingers scraping at my scalp as she whispers, "You insisted we were made for each other. And I believe you." Honey and apples. She surrounds me, she fills me. The bond thread sparkles and glows brighter. I realize it's the same color as the morning sun illuminating her hair as she says, "I love you, Vadasz."

CHAPTER 23

ANA

I think I've stunned my monster. But the longer he remains silent, the more panic and doubt creep in. Oh god, does he not love me? Did I read this wrong? Did he bring me back to the human realm to ...?

My hair whips me in the face as Vadasz moves inhumanly fast. In a blink, we are at the balustrade. He sits me on the stone railing, open space behind me, the sheer cliff below me. I clutch his shoulders as he kisses my neck, bending me backwards over the balcony he threw me off of a couple weeks ago. The lick of fear mixes with my arousal, and I moan as my shirt disappears. His fangs scrape my breast as his claws prick the skin of my back. When he sucks my nipple, I let my head fall back. "Asz."

"Yes, my little sprite. What do you want? What do you need?"

Being on this balcony, riding the line between fear

and pleasure, it's giving me ideas. Before I've fully formed my thoughts, I say, "Chase me."

He goes still, and his claws dig in a little deeper, drawing a moan from my lips. "Little sprite?"

My pussy clenches, and wetness drips down my inner thigh, smearing his skin where we're pressed together. Now that I've said the words, I need it. I need the primal side of my monster. "Chase me. Like that first time."

He pulls back, his eyes searching my face. "Do not tempt me with such things."

"I trust you."

I lift one leg, draping it over his hip, grinding into him as anticipation builds. Slowly, he slides me down his body, his eyes burning full white. Yes. My monster likes this idea very much. I'm getting wetter with every panted breath as we stare at each other under the starlight.

With a flick of his hand, I'm clothed, which isn't what I was expecting ... until I look down. The corset of my Halloween dress hugs my chest, and the tattered skirt swirls, tickling my thighs. The dress is clean, and the torn skirts are much shorter, but other than that, it's the same. When I reach up, I feel the braids in my hair, and I smile.

I gasp as his hand wraps around my waist, and I realize he's grown larger. He grins, flashing his fangs, his giant cock leaking pre-cum, the frills fluttering like the tendrils of a jellyfish. His voice is low and clear as she asks, "You trust me?" I swallow and nod. "And if things get ... too intense?"

He grips me tighter, and I rub my thighs together. "I'll say, moonlight."

He grins, slicking his long tongue up my neck. "Then, run, little sprite."

I'm airborne. Starlight surrounds me as the frigid mountain air bites my skin and tugs at my skirts. I hang for a long moment, holding his heated gaze. And then I fall. Tears stream from my eyes as the mountain whips by. Fear is like a live wire in my veins as anticipation thrums through me.

The ground gets closer, and closer, and closer. I'm not worried. I'm scared, but I'm not worried. A few feet before I hit, the familiar touch of his magic surrounds me, and I slow down. The moment my toes hit dirt, I run.

A branch scratches my cheek, but I barely notice the burn. A growl rumbles behind me, much too close. I'm not ready for this to end. Not yet. My palm stings as I grab a thin tree trunk to swing myself down a trail to my right. A stone digs into my heel, and I stumble, but keep running.

A shadow flies overhead, and I barrel into thicker brush, trying to conceal myself. I know there's no hiding from him, but I try.

"You can't escape me, little sprite." His voice whispers in the air to my left, but when I look, he's not there. My breath wheezes, and my lungs burn, but I keep running. I've never been so turned on.

I'm jerked to a stop, and I reach back with both hands, yanking on my skirts to free them from the bare branch. The fabric tears, and I take off.

The hunt continues.

I feel his breath on my neck. I catch glimpses of red, glowing eyes in the shadows. There's a brush of fur against my calf, and a gentle swipe of a claw down my back.

I run.

A clearing opens up ahead. The moonlight turns the grass a muted shade of silver. For some reason, that little field feels like safety, even though I know it's not. I race towards it. The close press of trees thins as I get closer, and I'm able to see more of the night sky.

My breath punches from my lungs as I'm tackled from behind. Arms wrap around me, taking the brunt of the fall, but rocks and roots still scrape at my shins and palms. He's caught me, but I'm not giving up. I've had a taste of this adrenaline-fueled pleasure, and I want more.

My fingers dig at the dirt as I scramble. I kick and drag myself out from under him, and he lets me go, but only for a second. A hand wraps around my ankle and pulls me back. With a growl, Vadasz flips me onto my back.

My monster is glorious. His dark skin glints in the silver moonlight, his eyes burn white with desire, and his tail thrashes behind him as he reaches for me. Digging my heels into the ground, I try to scoot myself backwards, but that earns me a hand around my neck, collaring me in place.

The moan that leaves my throat is involuntary, and I arch into his touch. He leans over me, pressing some of his body weight into me as he snaps his jaws in my face. "You thought you could escape me, little sprite?"

When I play at struggling under him, I jolt when the fabric of my dress cuts into my skin as he rips it, corset and all. I'm so turned on, the pain quickly melts into a deep, throbbing pleasure.

His voice cracks. "Mine."

Fuck. Yes.

I'm pushed into the dirt as he drives his cock inside me.

"Asz!"

"Ana!"

With primal grunts and growls, he pumps his length into me. Each thrust is hard and unforgiving. My inner thighs are going to bruise. I love it. I try to buck into him, but there's little room to move.

His body grows larger, and I scream. He holds me down, and as he continues to drive his cock into me, he unfurls his long tongue. Saliva drips onto my skin, and then he licks a long stripe from my belly button, between my breasts, and up my throat.

"Asz. Asz! I ... I'm going to—"

He pulls his cock out of me, his frills sucking and pulling at my pussy like they don't want to let go. I clench, but without his friction, I've lost the edge, and I fall away from the orgasm that was right there a moment ago.

Before I have the chance to whine, I'm flipped over. My cheek slams into the ground. I'm so high on the rush and the desire coursing through me, I don't feel pain, only more and more pleasure. As I take a stuttering breath, I cough, and a little cloud of dust puffs up. One of his hands presses my head down, keeping the side of my face pinned to the ground. I kick my legs, but it's no use.

"Gods, Ana. Look at you, my dirty little sprite writhing on the forest floor for me."

A knee pushes my thighs apart. I scream, swallowing dirt as he thrusts inside me. Can the other monsters of this realm hear my screams? Will they defy The Ancient One and come investigate? Will they try to take me from him?

I groan as I squirt all over the forest floor. Even if the monsters come, Vadasz would kill them. And gods, if that doesn't send my pussy pulsing with need.

His frills grip my clit, and I explode. Drool leaks from the corner of my mouth, turning the ground under my cheek to mud. I don't care. My body is electrified. Shocks of pleasure radiate from my pussy.

Before my orgasm has the chance to fade, his hand wraps around my throat as he rocks backwards. I'm lifted off the ground onto his lap, my back slamming to his chest. He licks my neck, and we both groan. He fucks up into me as his large palm tilts my head down. "Look at your perfect breasts bouncing in the starlight."

I've never particularly loved my breasts. I don't hate them, but they are small. Cute. I've never thought of them as sexy, until now. I'm smeared with dirt, scratches mark my skin, and my dress hangs from me in tatters. I've never felt hotter.

I reach down, playing my fingers over his frills as they pop and suck at my clit. My head falls back to his chest, and he grips my throat tighter. He curls over me, and our eyes meet. I say the words because I never want him to hold back like he did with her. Never again. "Come. I want to feel your release, Asz."

His thrusts stutter, and the growl he releases takes me with him. His frills stiffen inside me as he comes, and all I can do is gasp around his hand on my neck. He holds my gaze, and I hold his, as we fall apart together. My orgasm tears through me, and I whisper, "B-bite."

"Fuck, Ana." My vision turns white as his fangs sink into the mate mark on my neck. I scream as he bellows. His cum leaks out of me, and I run my fingers through it, bringing them to my lips. I lick our combined release, and he groans, his cock kicking inside me.

I shift, and he lets go of my throat. I feel his heartbeat against my back, and when I look down, our bond thread burns brighter.

My legs are shaky as I slide off him, and my hot blood drips down my chest. When I turn to face him, he leans forward, licking it away with a hum of pleasure. "Apples and honey."

I lean forward, and he hunches so I can bring my lips

to his. After a brief kiss, I smile up at him. "Smoke and snow."

His fingers scrape my scalp as he grips my hair. He holds me, his eyes searching. My gaze drops to his lap before snapping back to his face. I nod, and he shoves me onto his cock. I can't swallow all of him, but I take as much as I can until he hits the back of my throat. Tears burn as he grinds into my face, and I grip his thighs. His frills play with my tongue, and just when I've gotten used to his size, he pulls me back and thrusts.

As he fucks my mouth, I realize I'm about to come again.

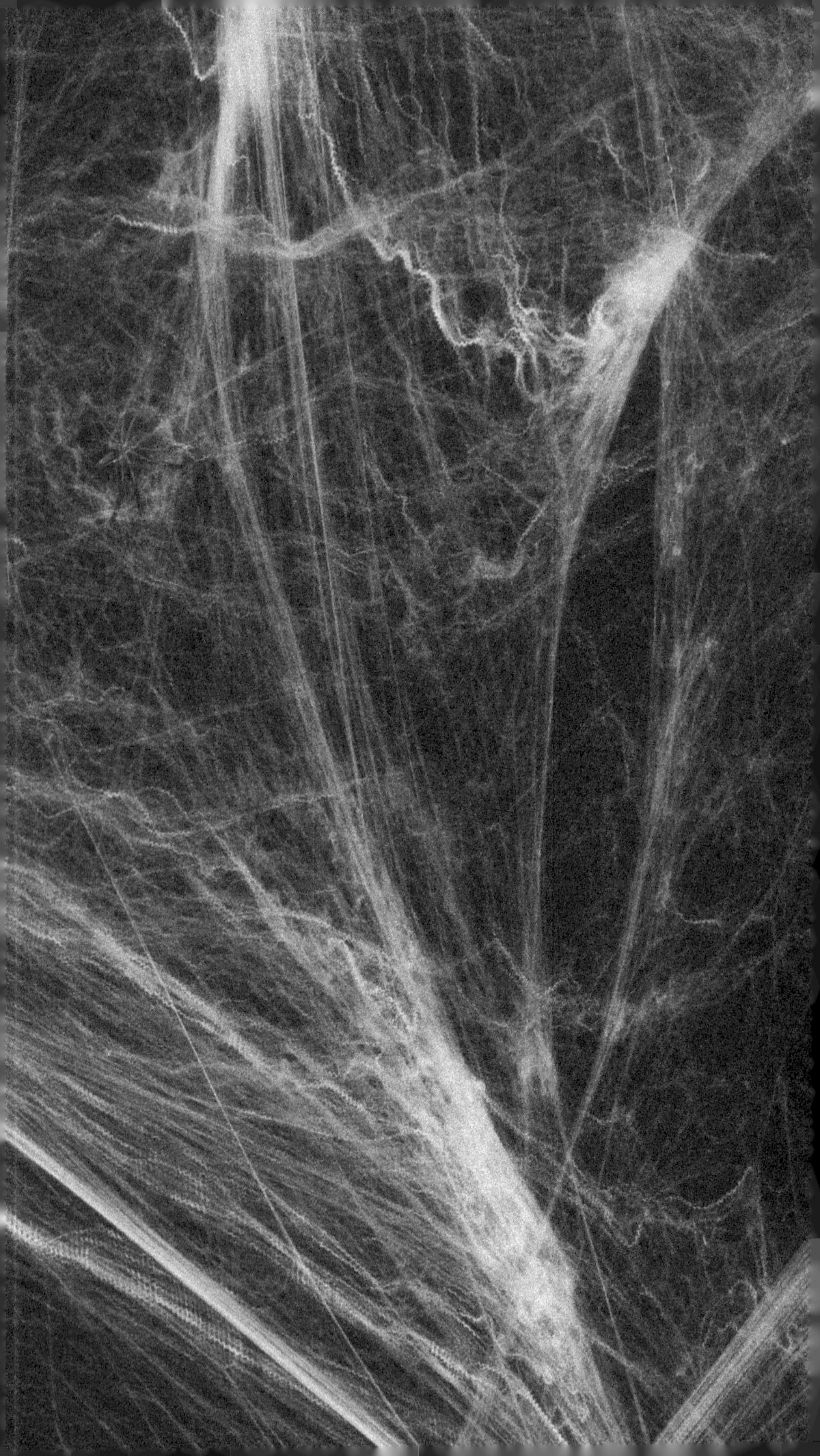

CHAPTER 24

VADASZ

What little control I have left, I use to make sure I don't hurt my little sprite. I've lost myself to her fantasies, but I must be careful. I could so easily break her.

My mate's mouth is spread wide to take me, and saliva drips down her chin. Her lips are swollen and red, and tears glisten in her eyes. She's perfect.

Ecstasy rolls through me. My entire body shakes with my orgasm, and though my eyes threaten to roll back, I can't look away. I watch Ana as I come, filling her mouth. She swallows, and the suction draws another rush of cum from me. She sputters, and my release leaks from her lips, but she swallows again. Before I come again, I pull her off me, and she takes a gasping breath. With one hand, I wipe her mouth before pressing little kisses to her face.

I nuzzle her neck and pull a portal around us, bringing us back to the balcony. Lifting my gaze to the sky, I expend a decent amount of magic to call a warm rain. When Ana gasps with a smile, then sighs, I know it was magic well spent.

Slowly, I peel the scraps of her dress off her body. My gaze follows the trails of rain as it washes away the dirt from her skin. I kiss a long red mark on her cheek before healing it. I lick at the little scrapes on her thighs, her stomach, her ass ...

The rain plasters her hair to her head, turning it a darker shade of red, like blood cooled on the steel of a sword. Little sprays of water escape her lips with each of her breaths, and I want to capture each one.

Wrapping my arms around her, I hold her in a tight hug. She hugs me back, burrowing her cheek against my chest. It's nice, just to be held. I stroke her back, inhaling her scent, which seems even more potent in the rain.

I don't realize I've tightened my grip until she pats my back, her voice muffled inside our hug. "Asz? What's wrong?"

I curl around her. "Nothing, little sprite. Nothing at all. Everything is perfect. You're perfect." She takes a deep breath, then relaxes into me. The words are there. I love her. It's a powerful word, but it's a small one. Only four letters. Can they hold everything I feel for my mate?

I'm an Ancient. I can do better.

"Ana, I want to show you the universe. There are countless realms I can access with my magic, and I would lay them all at your feet. I've lived a long time, and I've seen much. I used to think I'd seen too much, but now I want to start over ... with you. I want to see everything again through your eyes." I brush a tear off her smiling cheek. "Will you reintroduce me to everything, to everywhere, to ... life?"

She lunges forward, pressing her lips to mine. She smiles through the kiss before pulling away. "I can't wait."

I let go of the magic, and the rain stops. I stand, drying our skin and hair before wrapping a thick blanket around my mate. She snuggles into my arms as I sit on the over-sized chair, hugging her in my lap.

In the silence, I find I want to say the simple words after all. "I love you, Ana."

She curls her fingers against my chest, right over my heart, and I feel her love for me caress our bond—our gold thread glitters with it.

My fingers play with her hair as I lean back to let her lay against my chest. We watch the eternal night sky, and a shooting star streaks across the velvet backdrop. I whisper in her ear. "Make a wish."

"I don't have to. I have you."

I send up a prayer of apology and thanks to the Fates, because I feel the same way.

There is a secret project underway with these characters, so be sure you're subscribed to my newsletter and following me on social media so you don't miss out

Reviews are so so so important, especially for smaller authors like myself. Please leave a review. It doesn't have to be detailed ... even a simple star rating helps.

I genuinely hope you enjoyed this series. If you're interested, here are my other books - all adult fantasy with varying levels of spice.

Scan the code below for links to my Amazon author page where you'll find all my other books.

You'll also find a link to my website for signed paperbacks & hardcovers as well as swag.

ACKNOWLEDGMENTS

A huge thank you to my readers. Without you, this crazy dream of being an author would not be possible.

To all my beta & ARC readers, thank you! You had a big hand in making this series what it is today. Thank you so very much for taking the time to help me polish this story.

And lastly, I want to thank all my friends and family for cheering me on and being as excited about my characters as I am—I love my tribe.

ABOUT THE AUTHOR

T. B. Wiese is a military spouse, dog mom, photographer, Disney nerd, and lover of spicy fantasy. She loves animals (She grew up with dogs and working with horses, including working at the Tri-Circle D Ranch at Disney World), so don't be surprised when you find yourself reading lovable animal characters in her novels.

If you'd like to keep up to date with future releases as well as new swag and sales, sign up for her newsletter via link in code below.

SCAN THE CODE WITH YOUR CAMERA APP FOR HER SOCIAL LINKS

www.ingramcontent.com/pod-product-compliance
Lightning Source LLC
Chambersburg PA
CBHW070421310726
48977CB00003B/786